Sagebrush

D.L. Hatton

This is a work of fiction. All the characters and events in this book are either products of the author's imagination or are used fictitiously.

© 2006 By D.L. Hatton

ISBN: 978-0-6151-3877-0

Acknowledgments

Preparing a manuscript for publication is a bigger project than I knew. It has required many hours above and beyond my time or talents. Therefore I gratefully acknowledge the efforts of my wife. She has run our small business while I have put this book together. I thank my son Eric and for the many hours of computer work he put in setting up the formatting. My son Caleb has done the photography and cover design with the equipment he bought to further his career as film director, producer and actor.

I also wish to thank Keith Burris for scanning my manuscript and converting it to an electronic copy and for teaching me to use my computer in such a way as to eliminate many hundreds of hours work not only in this work but in many yet to come. Janine Bolon has also been a big help in getting me started in the publishing business.

Preface

Nicole, a bright and happy co-ed has her life turned up side down by the retirement, illness and death of her father. Extracted from the polite society of Boston and thrust rudely into the life of a working girl in a seedy second rate gambling house in a small Nevada town she meets the Weslys. The younger is handsome, rich, smooth and fun. The older is course, rough, eccentric and rebellious. The antics and rivalry of these two afford relief from her mundane stifling life.

Swept innocently along Nicole finds herself embroiled in a one man sagebrush rebellion. Old fashioned ideas clash with the new leaving Nicole in the middle of the road to be run over by traffic going both ways.

Chapter 1

Nicole pushed through the swinging doors that separated the kitchen from the dining room in the Wooden Nickel Bar and Casino. That very morning she had received her ninety day, end of probation interview with the owner.

"You have done very well in almost every area of our business. You learn quickly and you are much more ambitious than the other girls," old Singletree had complimented. Her hopes for the promised raise were reinforce".

"However," he had continued, "in our business the customer is king. I hired you to be friendly with the men, encourage them to drink more, gamble more, eat more, and leave more money, preferably, all their money. You are one classy looking little broad. You could bring us a lot more business if you weren't so stiff and formal".

"They paw me if I'm friendly," she protested.

"Watch the other girls. They are very friendly but they don't allow attentions they don't want."

Nicole had watched them work and knew he spoke the truth but she had never been able to imitate them. Her raise had been in keeping with the pernicious old man's character. He had promised more if she would 'loosen up.'

"Stingy bastard," She felt ashamed immediately. Her language was deteriorating to match those around her.

The customer at table ten was drunk, as were his buddies even though the sun had barely gone down. He had stroked the back of her leg when she had served them dinner and patted her fanny as she had turned to go. He laughed as she had moved lightly away. He was showing off for his friends. She had tried to flirt and be friendly like the others would have done, but it only made him more aggressive.

It was wearing on her nerves and now she must return to their table to serve another round of drinks. She stepped to the bar and took the tray that Singletree placed before her. With a great effort she managed to smile as she placed a drink next to each costumer, serving Rhino last. She had chosen this nickname for him for his resemblance to that animal. It was a mistake. He jerked her down onto his lap without fear of spilling the drinks. He leaned her back and her legs came up, her short skirt hiding very little. His kiss missed her mouth, and was placed on the side of her chin. He tipped her back up and released her. His friends laughed as she retreated behind the bar.

"Don't look so upset. They didn't do any harm, just having a little fun," Singletree admonished.

Two more customers had come in and approached the bar. One was tall, broad shouldered with deep chest, but he moved with a loose jointed motion of uncommonly long arms and legs. He was dark of hair, eye and complexion, with a jutting beetle brow. He looked formidable. His companion was a couple of inches shorter with the same broad shoulders and deep chest, but was perfectly proportioned and handsome. He was fairer of skin and had reddish brown hair. Strangely, there was a strong resemblance between the two. They had to be brothers with maybe a ten years difference in age, the handsome one being the younger. He looked like a nice guy. Nicole smiled at him without much effort.

"Go back to the cooler in the kitchen and bring some sweet cider," Singletree ordered.

When she returned, the younger man was sipping a beer. She was ordered to pour a big glass of cider for the older. In the back ground Nicole could hear an argument from Rhino's table.

"I won the bet fair and square."

"No you didn't. You had to surprise her. She didn't do it willingly."

"I kissed her didn't I?"

"Yeah, on the chin."

"What does that matter? She wanted it. Didn't you see her smiling at me?"

Rhino, looking disgusted, arose and made his way to the hat rack behind the door. Nicole tried to dally behind the bar until he was gone, but Singletree, indicating a full tray to be served, waved her away with his finger. Rhino was directly in her way as she came around the end of the bar. He stepped back to let her pass next to the wall. His arm shot out directly in front of her chest and was planted firmly against the wall. Immediately she tried to step back but he had anticipated this move. His other arm trapped her as he stepped close.

"Leave her alone," The sound was like a boom box reaching every corner of the room. Rhino's massive head swung menacingly.

"Now Wes," Singletree moved quickly around the end of the bar.

"Now Wes, let's not get in trouble over a barmaid," The younger man closed ranks with Singletree.

Rhino grinned and swung back to Nicole. With his massive body he pinned her to the wall and with his hand clamped over her jaw from beneath, he kissed her roughly on the mouth. She bit his lip. Jerking his head back, his hand went to his injury. She almost squirmed loose but his hand caught her by the breast and squeezing and twisting he slammed her against the wall. She yelped in pain. Abruptly her tormentor was jerked away from her, and smashed back the other way into the door, his head breaking the wood and glass of the small individual panes. The head pitched forward imitated by the rest of the body that ended up in a heap on the floor. The man called Wes stood flexing and shaking his skinned bleeding knuckles.

"Damn, it must be solid clear through," he described Rhino's head.

Nicole, with arms before her, was hunched against the pain.

"Get your coat, sweetheart, I'll give you a ride home," Wes directed. She left to comply.

"Wes," the younger man protested. "I've got a date. You promised me the truck."

"Wes," Singletree was protesting at the same time, "this ain't your affair! She works for me."

"She ain't suited to this kind of work. Cain't you see that?" Wes countered.

"She'll learn. She'll change."

"That would be a real shame," Wes silenced old Singletree.

When Nicole returned with her things, Rhino was gone and Singletree was sweeping up the glass. He gave her a hard stare. She had more than her coat in hand. It was plain that she wasn't coming back. Wes and his brother arose and accompanied her out to their pickup. The younger brother let her in and climbed in behind her. Wes would drive.

"I'll drop you off at Amy's," Wes said.
"I'll ride with you."

"I thought you were all in a sweat to see her," Wes needled.

"I'm not all in a sweat to sit and visit with her father for hell knows how long."

Without asking her for directions Wes pulled away from the curb and headed up the road. He turned at the right spot and sped up as they left town. Nicole looked out at the black night. How she hated this valley and the people in it. It looked so peaceful with only an occasional light in the distance from the scattered ranches to indicate life. She must have unconsciously reverted to the habit of talking to herself that she had fallen into in the last nine months.

"The people here are alright. You've only seen the grimy underside of the creature," Wes contradicted. "Many of them would give you the shirt off their back."

"Nobody has lifted a finger to help us," Nicole stated.

"You are just too proud to tell anybody you needed it, I haven't heard a thing."

"Why should you know anything about us?"

"I live in the valley," Wes' tone of voice indicted she must be a simpleton to have asked this question.

All the gossip that Nicole had heard at the Wooden Nickel came to mind. The valley was a deep gash in the desert floor averaging five miles in width. It was thirty miles long. Many springs turned this narrow strip into to a verdant very productive oasis. Most of the springs were near the northern end of the valley but drained toward the south making it possible to irrigate the whole valley. The next town was over a hundred miles away. The people having to depend on each other had become very clannish. Outsiders were accepted very slowly.

"The only money my mother and I had to live on came from the Wooden Nickel. That is the only place that would hire me."

Immediately Wes slowed the pickup. There being no speed limits between towns in the state, they had reached nearly eighty miles an hour. Seeing a small side road Wes tromped hard on the brake and with the vehicle sliding sideways he managed to pull off the road and stop.

"It will wait until tomorrow!" The young man protested.

"Old Turnbill is going on vacation tomorrow," Wes responded.

Wes shifted into reverse and backed the truck back onto the road.

"Wes!" The young man screamed.

Just in the nick of time Wes turned the steering wheel bringing the truck around into the southbound lane, facing back the way they had come as a vehicle went streaking by with horn blaring heading north. Almost instantly it was gone indicating the terrific speed at which it had been traveling.

"What are you howling about?" Wes asked calmly. "We had plenty of room."

"Someday Wes!" The threat wasn't finished as the young man leaned weakly back in his seat.

Turnbill turned out to be the banker. They were all sitting comfortably in his living room as Wes came directly to the point.

"This young lady is looking for work. I'd be much obliged if you would give her a try for a few weeks."

"I'd be glad to if she has any training but our customers expect professional, accurate service," Turnbill was eying with distaste Nicole's over painted face and skimpy attire. Her perfume was strong in the air.

"Does she do books?" Turnbill obviously thought that this requirement would absolve him from any responsibility to hire her.

"Certainly," Wes boomed out confidently.

"She won't have any trouble keeping track of the piddling amount of money you handle."

Turnbill still hesitated.

"Sometimes people need a break when they get their tail in the wringer," Wes looked significantly at the banker.

"Yes, I, er... she can start when I get back next Monday. I usually start my girls at four eighty an hour."

"Thank you, Rudy. I told her you were a generous person."

Turnbill's ears turned red.

"Perhaps if she is qualified or shows an aptitude for the work I can start her at a higher rate. A bank is a much more conservative establishment than a casino," Turnbill looked pointedly at Nicole's clothes.

"Yes, I understand perfectly. Thank you very much Mr. Turnbill," Nicole said sincerely.

"Trimble," the banker corrected with a scowl.

"Don't blame her. She's new here. Probably has never heard you called anything else," Wes excused her. Nicole noticed the young man next to her covering his smile with his hand. The interview was over. As they stood to leave Trimble, with a gesture, held Wes back and spoke softly.

"She didn't ever work down south did she?" His tone of voice indicated he was having second thoughts.

"Nope," Wes assured him.

"Wes, stop at the gas station, I better call Amy and explain things," The young man had examined Nicole closely during the interview with the banker. She was younger than he had first thought. Away from the cheap, faded imitation elegance of the Nickel he could see she was quite beautiful beneath the paint. Her figure was excellent. The thoughts of riding next to her the twenty miles to her ranch greatly appealed to him.

"Amy? I'm going to be late. Something has come up that is beyond my control."

Nicole had gotten out of the stuffy truck and walked up and down on the sidewalk in front of the phone booth to stretch her legs. She hadn't meant to eavesdrop but the young man had a strong voice.

"Wes picked up some pretty little barmaid. He is going to give her a ride home. She lives about fifteen minutes out. No, if I do that we may never see him again. I either go with him or we won't have wheels for the night."

The young man hung up and turned, his eyes met hers.

"Is Wes in the habit of picking up barmaids?" She wanted to know where she stood.

"No, as far as I know he's never done it before."

She was puzzled.

"You seemed to think Amy would accept that as a reasonable excuse."

"Everybody knows that Wes does what he wants when he wants for reasons that nobody else understands. I didn't mean to put you in a bad light but Amy is a very jealous type. I'm sure she will smell your perfume on me, our riding in a small cab together and all," He finished lamely.

"Yes, you better cover all the bases," She was amused. Wes once again sped down the road toward her home. "I want to thank you Mr..."

"Wesly, Lionel Wesley."

"You have been very kind."

He waved away her thanks. Her gratitude embarrassed him.

"I'm Richard Wesley," The young man made sure she knew his name.

"Likes to be called Dicky," Wes informed her.

"Dicky?" Nicole turned to see a pained look on Richard's face.

It was obviously a hated nickname. Wes chuckled. Richard fidgeted and squirmed in the confined space. She moved to give him more room. He then stretched and settled back to get comfortable his arm falling back along the seat behind her. He shifted in the name of comfort and was once again close to her. She smiled to herself at his antics.

"Do you ride?" he asked very casually.

"Ride?"

"Horses."

"I've ridden a little. I'm not very good at it."

"Maybe I could come over and give you some lessons sometime."

"That would be nice," she answered politely.

"You'd look mighty pretty dressed in Levis and western shirt sitting on a horse. With a nice sun tan you'd look right at home," Richard was talking softly.

She wondered if he was merely daydreaming or if he was hinting that she would be acceptable if she dressed and was tanned like the other girls in the valley. Richard shifted again. She could feel the warmth of his arm touching her neck and shoulders.

"There's a coyote!" There was excitement in Wes' voice. He brought the truck gently to a stop. He quietly stepped out, drawing a rifle from a sheath in front of the seat behind their legs.

"That isn't a coyote. That is a broken off fence post," Richard was irritated at the interruption. All Nicole could see was an elongated dot in the distance at the further reaches of the lights. Wes' rifle spoke. The dot disappeared.

"Got him!" Wes exclaimed.

"Missed him," Richard contradicted at the same moment. Wes put his rifle away and they drove on down the road. The passed the spot where Nicole thought the dot had been.

"Missed him," Richard sounded satisfied.

They drove slowly on for another short distance.

"Well now, look at that, a large male post lying dead along side the road," Wes pointed at the coyote. "Pelt is worth seventy dollars," he explained.

"If it was winter," Richard pointed out.

"There's still the bounty."

"I thought you told me there was no longer a bounty?"

Wes didn't answer but sped up and drove past the carcass. Richard smiled in victory. He was sore at Wes for interrupting his courting. Nicole suspected Wes had deliberately set out destroy the romantic mood Richard was cultivating.

"What is down south that Mr. Trimble doesn't like?" she asked Wes.

"Whore house, Singletree owns it. It's those trailers that sit around that park by the lake at the south end of the valley. Some of the gals got their start at the Wooden Nickel."

"I see," She shuddered.

They arrived at her home with no further incidents. Richard walked her to the door. He asked her for a date to go riding which she accepted.

Chapter 2

Nicole sat in the courtroom nervously fingering her purse. It contained a subpoena to appear as a witness in Frieker vs. Wesly, an assault and battery case. Her mother sat next to her. Beside the criminal action, Frieker was suing for damages and court costs. The plaintiff's lawyer was quick to put Rhino on the stand.

"What were you doing when Mr. Wesly hit you?"

"Flirting with the barmaid."

"Had you done anything to provoke Mr. Wesly?"

"Absolutely nothing."

"What possible motive could he have had?"

"He must have been jealous. She was quite pretty."

"He had no way of knowing what I was thinking," Wes spoke up.

"Objection sustained," The judge concurred.

Next pictures showing the plaintiff's face were shown as evidence. It was all twisted and discolored. Photos of the back of his head showed the hair shaved off and a long crooked gash. A Dr. Swenson testified that these wounds were made the night Rhino had been in the bar. Rhino had lost two teeth, suffered a broken jaw and had eleven stitches in his head. Next Singletree was called to the stand.

"Now sir, would you tell the court what happened."

"It happened just like he said," Singletree motioned indicating Rhino.

"Tell it in your own words please."

"This feller here," again he indicated Rhino, "was flirting with the girl here at the end of the bar. They had been flirting back and forth all evening. Suddenly for no good reason, Wes told him to lay off or something similar, then Wes stands up."

"And what did you do?"

"I stepped around the end of the bar and me and Richard stepped between this feller and Wes."

"Richard?"

"Yes, Richard Wesly."

"Why did you do that?"

"Everyone knows Wes has a temper."

"Even a member of his own family tried to stop him?"

"That's right."

"What happened next?"

"He just flung us aside. He's incredibly strong."

"When you say he, you mean the defendant?"

"Yes."

"What happened next?"

"He grabbed this feller here and spun him around and punched him."

"How many times?"

"I couldn't rightly say."

"What happened then?"

"This feller here smashed his head into the window in the door then flopped on the floor, out cold. He never got up."

"What did the defendant say at this time?"

"He said, 'Come on honey, let's go.' It was obvious he was sweet on her."

"Singletree, you damned liar. That ain't how it was!" Wes was on his feet.

"Wes! Er .. Mister Wesly, I'll have no further outbursts in this court room. You will have your chance to cross-examine. Mr. Singletree, you will confine your testimony to the facts. You will not state your opinion. Is that clear?"

"Yes, your honor."

"Mr. Trimble," The plaintiff's counsel began questioning the next witness, "Would you please describe what occurred in your front room the night of the incident."

"Wes brought Nicole by to meet me."

"For what purpose?"

"She was in need of a job."

"So Wes brought Nicole straight from the casino to you asking for a job for her?"

"I guess."

"Did you hire her?"

"I did."

"Had you ever seen this gal before?"

"No."

"On what basis did you decide to hire her?"

"Wes seemed to place great confidence in her."

"Would you say that he knew her well?"

"I'm sure he did."

By the time the plaintiffs case had been presented the jury was looking unfavorably at Wes. Wes called Nicole to the witness chair. She was sworn in. She sat looking innocent and wholesome. She was tanned and dressed like any other rancher's daughter in the valley. All this had been done upon Richard's advice. He had been over to her place several times. She had come to like and trust him despite the fact he considered himself a playboy.

Mr. Trimble, sitting with the spectators trying to look optimistic, gave her the thumbs up.

"Miss Defoe had you and I met before the night in question?"

"No."

"Would you describe to the court what happened?"

"The plaintiff had been harassing me all night. Finally he positioned himself so he could trap me as I went by. He grabbed me and forced a kiss on me."

"Was it then that he got violent?"

"Objection your honor. The defense is leading the witness."

"Sustained, rephrase the question Mr. Wesly."

"What happened then?"

"I bit him. He shoved me against the wall

17

and he hurt me badly."

"Were you badly bruised?"

"Yes."

"May I make a statement at this time?"

The plaintiff's counsel agreed to let Wes make his statement after being sworn in as a witness.

"I interfered on Nicole's behalf only after the plaintiff seized her by the breast and caused her to cry out in pain."

"Miss Defoe," the cross examination began,

"You have testified that you bit Mr. Frieker."

"Yes."

"Where did you bite him?

"On the lip."

"Would agreed that such a bite would be very painful?"

"I assume so."

"Did you wait on the plaintiff's table?"

"Yes."

"Did you smile at him?"

"Yes, but..."

"Did you sit on his lap?"

"He pulled me down before…"

"But you did sit on his lap."

"Yes but…"

"Yes, but what Miss Defoe?"

"Mr. Single tree ordered me to be friendly with the customers but Rhino was harassing me."

"Who was harassing you Miss Defoe?"

"The plaintiff."

"So you were smiling and flirting with the plaintiff but when he got friendlier than you wanted him to, you bit him."

"Yes."

"At what point did Mr. Wesly come in?"

"I didn't see him come in."

"I submit you didn't see him come in because you were sitting on the plaintiff's lap."

"Your honor, counsel for the plaintiff is trying to color the witnesses' testimony. She said she didn't see me come in."

"Point well taken. Counselor, don't make conclusions for the court."

"Miss Defoe, Mr. Wesly says he interfered when you screamed. You did scream didn't you?"

"I don't think I screamed but I must have made some noise to..."

"You must have, Miss Defoe?"

"He was hurting me. That's what I know!"

"Did a doctor examine your bruise?"

"No

"Did you show it to your mother?"

"No."

"How did Mr. Wesly know you had a bruise?"

"I mentioned it to Richard."

"But no one saw it?"

"No."

Counsel for the plaintiff had no more questions for Nicole. Wes was called to the stand for cross-examination.

"Mr. Wesly, did you see Miss Defoe sitting on the plaintiff's lap?"

"Yes."

"At what point did you lose control and punch Mr. Frieker?"

"I didn't lose control."

"So you calmly battered Mr. Frieker without anger?"

"Being angry and losing control isn't necessarily the same thing!"

"Thank you Mr. Wesly."

Counsel for the plaintiff in his closing argument said in part;

"Ladies and gentlemen of the jury, the witnesses for the plaintiff tell a consistent and cohesive story. Testimony bears out the fact that upon speaking to Miss Defoe the defendant used endearing and familiar phrases suggesting to the mind that they were closely associated. Testimony by our good banker strengthens this point. What man goes to an important man's home and solicits a job for a barmaid he has never seen before?

Testimony supports the fact the defendant watched as Miss Defoe at first flirted with the plaintiff but upon knowing that the defendant had entered the casino, she tried to put the plaintiff off. By testimony the defendant has admitted to attacking the plaintiff when he became angry. Two men were not enough to contain him. May I submit to the jury that the defendant attacked the plaintiff in a fit of jealous rage?"

Wes in his final argument was only able to rehash testimony given by himself and Nicole. There was little hope if the jury didn't believe them. The jury returned after a short deliberation. The foreman stood.

"Your Honor, we have reached a verdict. We find the defendant guilty as charged. However, because of extenuating circumstances we recommend leniency by the court.

"Court will be adjourned until three this afternoon when the defendant will be sentenced."

The courtroom was full to see what Wes would get.

"Lionel Wesly, you are sentenced to ninety days in jail. You will pay the defendant damages and court costs. Upon recommendation of the jury your jail sentence is hereby suspended. Damages and court costs amount to eighty-five hundred dollars to be paid to the court on behalf of Mr. Frieker."

"I'll not pay that drunken son of a bitch one damned dime!" Wes had spoken calmly enough but his big voice boomed through the court room. All went deathly quiet waiting to see what the judge would do.

"Mr. Wesly, you will change your attitude or you will do time."

"Send me up then."

"Six months in the county jail."

Nicole waited around until the courthouse was nearly empty, then she went to find Wes. She found Richard waiting in the hall.

"I've got to talk to Wes. I feel horrible about this. If it hadn't been for me..."

"Nonsense, listen," He took her by the arm and signaling her to be quiet, he walked her closer to an open door.

"Wes, for an intelligent man you do some of the stupidest things. When are you gonna learn?" It was the judge's voice. "Any competent lawyer could have won this case for you, but no, you think you know everything. Don't be so damned independent."

"Don't you remember Stephanie?"

"Of course I do."

"When she got through with me I was half skinned. My lawyer skinned the other half and left me to bleed to death.

"Alright, I'll grant you that but if you serve as your own counsel at least get someone to advise you and for hell's sake, prepare."

"I was in the right. It looked like an open and shut case."

"You might have been but . . . ."

"Might have been? What would you have done?"

"If I had been in your place I'd have punched him out too . . . if I had been physically able, but that isn't what I meant. You could have called Richard to testify. He could have been drawn out with the right questions to support your case. Old Turnbill thinks Nicole is the greatest thing on earth with the possible exception of gold bullion. He would have done a lot to elevate her from barmaid to respectable citizen with the right guidance. Frieker was so drunk at the time you could have torn his testimony apart. It's not enough to be right you have to be prepared."

"What do I do now?"

"You go to jail."

"You were a little hard on me, weren't you?"

"Wes you knot head, I did everything I could for you. The jury did everything they could but you screwed it up so bad we had little choice. Everyone enjoyed seeing Frieker get his, even counsel for the plaintiff. People like you, Wes. They don't understand you and are afraid of you but most think you are decent. If only you'd tone down a little."

"Are you afraid of me?"

"Not a bit.

"It's good to have someone understand."

"I didn't say that. Don't look so glum Wes. If you behave yourself you might get out in sixty days."

"What about the settlement? Isn't it still in force?"

"Sure, but I suspect Frieker may think that your sentence replaced the settlement."

"His counsel seemed pretty sharp."

"Yes, but I think he may take his nice fat check for winning the case and go on his way leaving Frieker in dark."

"Frieker will never collect in any case," Wes vowed.

"No, I don't think he will," The judge agreed.

"Who is Stephanie?" Nicole quizzed Richard.

"Wes' ex."

As they heard footsteps nearing the door Nicole and Richard moved away. Nicole tried to apologize to Wes but he waved her apology away. She had chosen an awkward place to try to speak to him. Her mother had watched the encounter. On their way home she voiced the opinion that Nicole's defender was an ill mannered ruffian who probably got involved merely because of an inclination to fight.

Chapter 3

Slowly Nicole's opinion of the valley', as it was referred to by the natives, began to change for the better. Still, she couldn't help but compare it to her former life. She missed the college dorms and her roommates. She missed the concerts and dances. She longed to fulfill her dream of becoming an interior decorator. She had nearly completed her degree and had even been interviewed for work in her field when disaster had struck. Her father had retired and decided he would like to run a modest sized ranch. He had promised to see that Nicole had her opportunities. Reno, to the north of them, was expanding rapidly and would offer abundant work in her field.

Not having done any ranching since he was a teenager there was much her father hadn't understood. His retirement income was used to make necessary improvements and to operate the ranch. Their finances had seemed solid although their cash flow had diminished. His stroke, followed a few weeks later by his death, had been so unexpected and devastating that her mother even yet had not been reconciled to it. To pay for utilities and food it was necessary for someone to get a job. Her mother had pleaded with her not to leave her alone and seek work outside the valley. They weren't in danger of losing the ranch but there was little extra. Her mother, fearful of even another move, had been reluctant to put the ranch up for sale. Each passing day she was becoming more adjusted to and comfortable in their present life.

With each passing day Nicole had felt more trapped and more resentful. Did her mother expect her to stay at home and work for the rest of her life, to forget her own dreams, to grow old without experiencing life? If only her mother would marry again.

It was at this point that the Weslys had come into her life. Richard had been attentive in his courting. Her mother liked him and had invited him to stay for dinner several times. His manners were impeccable, his wit sharp. It was good to hear laughter in the house again. She learned that he had been raised mostly in Reno. She also learned that he liked the girls from the valley. They were less sophisticated and were quite susceptible to his romancing. He had assumed that she, being from the valley, would fall into this category also.

Her mother, being many years younger than her father, was still quite attractive. Nicole for sometime had felt that her mother had married for security although she did have affection for her father. It occurred to her that Wes would only be eight or ten years younger than her mother. She had gotten the impression that Wes was well off. She also knew that he had been alone for sometime. Maybe, just maybe, she could get a romance going and be free from the responsibility to provide for her mother. Discouraging as her mother's comments about Wes had been, Nicole felt sure she would change her mind if she got to know him. He wasn't nearly as polished as Richard but he had a way of growing on you. Besides, he was the only prospect that she knew.

She had grown to enjoy her job with old Turnbill. At first he had been skeptical of their arrangement. She felt he kept an eye on her to keep her from stealing the money, but over time he had come to trust her. Although Wes had known nothing about her when he promised old Turnbill so much, it was true that she had no difficulty in doing all that she was asked with a minimum of instruction. He had given her a raise with the comment;

"You are quite efficient and you don't bug me all the time about unimportant things."

"Thank you. Wes was right, you are a generous person."

By the time Wes had come to trial they were fast friends.

Her conscience pricked her. She owed all the positive changes in her life to Wes. She hadn't been to the jail to see him in three weeks. Nicole was ushered into a small room that contained three cubicles. Each contained a stool and phone. A room` almost identical to it was on the other side of a solid glass partition. Wes was brought in and the door was locked behind him. He looked pale and unhappy. His face brightened momentarily as he saw her but his shoulders slumped once again as he sat down on his side of the glass. He picked up the phone in his cubicle.

"Hello sweetheart," he greeted her.

Nicole smiled. He greeted all young ladies this way. He used the same tone of voice that her grandfather used to use when he spoke to her.

"Hello Mr. Wesly."

"Wes, Dammit. None of this Mr. Wesly; makes me feel old."

"Are you getting along alright?"

"The food's rotten. Ya can't sleep decent for fear some damn criminal will murder you in your sleep or steal you blind. There's nobody with whom you can have a decent conversation. They are all a bunch of liars. I'm the only guilty one in the whole damned place to hear them talk. I admit what I done."

"I didn't know it was so bad."

"That ain't the half of it. I am so bored I could cry. The air is stuffy all the time. I feel like I'm suffocating."

"I wish there was something I could do."

"There is," Wes lowered his voice. "Bring me a small bomb disguised as a cake." His face had a wicked expression. Her face must have registered shock.

"Just kidding sweetheart. You hear that you bastards? I'm just joking. They monitor us when we have visitors." he explained. "If I wanted to escape I'd be out of here in an hour. All I want is a bomb for is a little excitement. You people are dull! You have no sense of humor," Wes was yelling into the phone. He motioned her to put her phone back to her ear.

"Now they know what I think of them maybe they'll hang up and let us talk in peace," He spoke quietly.

"Oh, Wes I'm so sorry, I..."

"Don't start that again," He cut her off brutally.

"I wish there was something I could do." She repeated awkwardly.

"Just talk to me. Tell me what's going on outside. Tell me about your life, anything, just talk to me."

"Richard and I..."

"Richard? That ungrateful pup hasn't been in to see me for a month I don't want to hear about him."

Nicole couldn't think of anything.

"How's your mother?" Wes asked.

"Fine."

"Nice looking woman."

"I'll tell her you said so. You made an impression on her too," Nicole carefully worded her response to avoid a lie.

"Is that right?" Wes looked pleased.

"We would like to invite you out to dinner at our place as soon as you get out."

"Thank you, Sweetheart. That's mighty nice of you. Tell your mother I'd be delighted."

Richard came by the bank to see her a few days later.

"I hope you've been to see Wes. He wasn't very happy with you the last time I saw him," She told him.

"He ought to be happy now. He's had a chance to chew my ear off. He expects me to do all the work at the ranch then drive all the way into town just to see him. He doesn't want me wasting time chasing the girls or having a beer or nothing. I'm not like him. I can't sit out there day after day, night after night and not go stir crazy."

"Speaking of stir crazy, Wes says he can't sleep nights because he's afraid of the inmates."

Richard began to laugh. The more he thought about it the funnier it seemed. He laughed harder until he had tears in his eyes.

"What's so funny?" Nicole wanted to know.

"While I was over at the jail just now..." Richard chuckled some more, "the deputy told me all the men in Wes' cell block are terrified of him. Everyone has asked to be transferred out."

"I'll stop by this evening when I get off work and tell him so he won't have to worry."

"Don't. It will be good for his character."

"Sometimes I get the feeling you and Wes

have a hard time getting along."

"I've hated Wes all my life, but now that I've been around him some I don't know. . . . there is some thing appealing about him....he's like a big kid. Some of the things he does drive me crazy but there is no malice in him."

"You weren't raised with Wes?"

"Only until I was about three. I went to live with mother. Wes stayed here."

"Divorce?"

"Yeah."

"That's always tough on kids. Are there any other kids in the family?"

"I have a sister just younger than I. She's eighteen."

"How old are you? I had the impression you were quite a bit older than that."

"I am." Richard avoided telling his age.

"How much older?"

Richard gave up knowing Nicole wouldn't be put off.

"I'm twenty."

"Twenty. That's a nice age. Why didn't you want to tell me?"

"You're twenty three," Richard confessed his reason uncomfortably.

"I see. I don't remember telling you my age."

"I asked around. Look Nicole, I came by to ask you to lunch not to discuss my age."

"Let me check something first," She pulled

him close by his ear and examined it closely.

"What are you doing? Making sure my ears are clean before you'll eat with me?"

"No, I was checking behind to see if they were still wet."

"Nicole!" Richard was insulted. He could hear her chuckling as she went to tell Turnbill she was leaving for lunch. They were close enough to walk to the Corner Cafe. Nicole was enjoying the cooler days of early fall. She looked around her at the beauty of the green fields and tall trees planted to shade the houses and town from the merciless summer sun. Even the starkness of the desert in the distance on both sides was beginning to appeal to her. She realized that her attitude had begun to change the day the Weslys had come into the Wooden Nickel. She said as much to Richard.

"My life has changed for the better since that day too," He looked knowingly into her eyes. She hadn't meant exactly the same thing he did, but she didn't disillusion him. After lunch he walked her back to the bank. Being a few minutes early Richard pulled her behind the hedge beneath the low hanging branches of a big tree that shaded the bank and tried to kiss her. She evaded him.

"A bank is a much more conservative establishment than a casino," she told him. "When you are a little older and have had more experience you will know that."

Richard rolled his eyes in exasperation.

"Come on Nicole, when are you going let

up?"

Nicole's sweet laughter filled the cozy nook. She kissed him then, slowly and carefully. He taken off guard for a second, responded with enthusiasm.

"Hmmmmm," Nicole made a sound in her throat as they finished. "No lack of experience there. Who taught you to kiss like that, Amy?"

"Nicole, are you jealous?" Richard was pleased at the thought.

Actually she wasn't but she didn't enlighten him.

"I hear you are still seeing her."

"I've known Amy a long time. It's not like I'm in love with her or anything, but it's hard to be mean to her. And she . . .well, to be honest she chases me. I've tried to hint but she's kinda' dense that way. I don't want hurt her feelings. She's more like a little sister, ya know?"

"Sure I understand completely. She's like a kissing cousin."

"Yeah,...no!"

"She sure is a pretty little thing."

Richard looked at her closely trying to evaluate her mood while desperately thinking of something to say.

"I haven't been spying on you. Everybody, and I do mean everybody, comes into the bank, even Linda. Is she a relative too?"

Richards face was stricken. He looked away in defeat. Nicole kissed him again, slowly and carefully.

"Hmmm, you do know how to kiss," She turned and walked sprightly into the bank.

Chapter 4

The Judge had been right. Wes was released early, his record having been without blemish while in jail. Nicole made the necessary arrangements for Richard and Wes to come out to the ranch for dinner as she had promised Wes.

They arrived a few minutes late. Her mother was irritated. While they had lived in Boston they had entertained often, their friends being the more affluent, well established families. Manners were impeccable, the food served at the right time, at the right temperature and in the right combinations. The wine was always appropriate. They, being French, enjoyed the tradition of fine entertaining.

Nicole always felt that it was her father's sense of humor that had prevented her mother from becoming a snob. Now that influence was gone.

"Mother, may I present Mr. Lionel Wesly."

"How da do, Ma'am," Wes offered his big hand. He pumped the hand offered him once in a gentle but abrupt motion then dropped it.

"Wes, this is my mother Gabriella Defoe."

"Charmed, I'm sure," Gabriella said with the slightest trace of sarcasm.

Wes didn't notice. Mrs. Defoe quickly seated the guests at table already fearing that the food was ruined. Not that she thought Wes would notice, but she did like Richard. There wasn't much conversation during the first part of the meal. Richard was embarrassed by Wes' lack of polish. Nicole was nervous hoping that Wes wouldn't think her mother a snob. The two younger people tried valiantly to sustain a conversation but Mrs. Defoe was still irritated and Wes was too busy eating.

"Good food," Wes complimented. "They oughta get you to cook at the Corner Cafe or the Nickel."

"Do you know the difference between a chef and a cook?" Mrs. Defoe spoke politely but there was frost all around the edges of her voice.

"Let me see, I've heard that one before...... tattoos, a chef ain't got tattoos" Wes laughed. Richard was embarrassed, Mrs. Defoe pursed her lips, and Nicole laughed in spite of herself.

"Sorry." She apologized in response to her mother's quick but cold glance.

"I'm sure you don't have tattoos," Wes said.

The dinner continued to drag through one disaster after another. The only one having a good time was Wes. Nicole quickly accepted the opportunity to step outside for some fresh air with Richard. Nothing she could do would salvage the evening.

"Bull in a china shop," Richard critiqued Wes' performance.

"Pretty awful wasn't it? I don't mean just

Wes. I mean the situation in general. In a way it isn't Wes who is the more impolite."

"What do you mean?"

"He is perfectly well mannered according to the customs here in the valley. Mother is the alien here yet she would impose her standard on Wes and call him rude while she looks down her nose. Wes has ignored every rudeness mother has thrown at him and continues to be polite."

"It's all gone right over his head," Richard said in disgust. "No." He held up his hand to silence her protest. "Let's not let them spoil our evening. Let's think about us." Richard drew her off the veranda that ran the length of the house into the shadows of the huge trees that surrounded the yard. Richard loved the trees that the pioneers had planted in every spot not needed for cultivation. This was the first time he had felt safe to bring Nicole here. The only good thing about bringing Wes tonight was the certainty that he would keep Mrs. Defoe occupied.

"What shall we talk about?" Richard put his arms around Nicole.

"Let's not, let's kiss," Nicole was amused at Richard. He would kiss a pretty girl at the drop of a hat but to talk about it so blatantly embarrassed him.

"Ummmm," she sighed, "I see you have been staying in practice."

"Nicole, about those other girls…"

"Hush," She put her hand over his mouth. She knew full well he had spent a lot of time to

37

prepare an explanation for a moment such as this.

"I don't want to hear it. Teach me more. I liked to be prepared."

"Prepared for what?"

She kissed him to avoid an answer. After a short and pleasant respite from the tension inside, Nicole lead Richard back into battle. To their surprise Wes was talking steadily to a very interested Mrs. Defoe. The subject was cattle raising in a desert habitat. It was obvious that Wes knew a great deal on the subject. Nicole was interested at first but soon got bored. Evidently, so did Richard.

"Why don't do those things on your own place?" He finally interrupted.

"One time a young kid fresh out of college came by with some information on how he could help me double my production on my farm and with my cattle. I told him I didn't need his help because I was only doing half of what I already knew," Wes laughed hard at his own joke. Nicole laughed more at Wes than the joke. Even her mother smiled.

"Didn't get it," Wes nodded at Richard's solemn face.

"I got it. It just wasn't funny," Richard defended. Before the two men left, Mrs. Defoe had accepted an offer from Wes to come over and help reorganize the program for the ranch to try and put it on a more profitable basis. They left the house and started down the long walk to the driveway. Catching the hint of smugness on her daughter's face at how the evening had turned out Mrs. Defoe spoke.

"He may know a lot about cattle but he will never understand fine dining. He ate like a horse."

At that precise moment Wes' faint but distinct voice drifted back to them from the parking lot.

"I didn't say I didn't like French cooking, Richard. I just said they overcook everything just a little bit."

Several days later Wes drove up to the house to make good on his word. Richard was with him to make time with Nicole. Wes went to talk to the ranch manager.

"I don't think this will work out very well," Nicole confided to Richard.

"Why not?"

"Our manager is real touchy about anyone telling him what to do. He only listens to mother because he has to. Even then he does what he likes once he thinks she isn't looking. I don't know what mother was thinking when she accepted Wes' offer."

"Maybe she is looking for a way to fire him. If he had a big fight with Wes she would have a good reason to send him down the road."

Loud laughter and coarse guffaws caused them to turn. The manager and two or three other men were all looking at Wes with glee. Wes had a strange little smile on his face like he had done something noteworthy.

"I don't like the looks of this," Richard declared. "Let's go find out what's going on."

Before they had taken two steps, Wes broke away from the group and approached them.

"I'm going out west to the see what shape the winter range is in. Do you two want to go? It's a pretty drive."

"Sure." Nicole answered.

"Nicole, I think it would be better to stay here."

"Why? I'd like to see it. I've never been out there."

"Trust me," Richard gave Wes a significant look.

"What's the matter Richard, 'fraid I'll make you work?" Wes chided.

"No. But ..."

"Then shut yer yap and get in. The little lady wants to go."

Wes and Nicole climbed into the pickup. An unhappy Richard was forced to get in or miss out on Nicole's company. Soon they were climbing out of the valley onto the high sagebrush mesa west of town. The mountains rose before them.

"How far away are they?" Nicole asked. Thirty miles," Wes told her, "of nothing but mile after mile of desert. It's real pretty in the spring. It greens up for a couple of months, then the flowers bloom, and then everything dries up again."

Wes drove for a couple of hours in a big circle. He stopped once in a while and walked out through the short brush to check the grass. There was precious little of it as far as Nicole could see. They stopped at a spring for a cold drink that fed a pretty little pond with crystal clear cool water. Not far past the spring Wes suddenly cried out.

"There's a coyote!"

"Where?" Richard asked.

"It just went behind that knoll!" Wes turned the pickup off the road and raced down into a swell toward the knoll.

"Look out Wes! It looks..." Richard had shouted too late. The pickup came quickly to a stop and slowly sank up to the axles. ".. boggy," Richard finished.

"Damn," Wes swore. "If you got some thing to say, spit out. Don't sit there and stutter. Now look what you got us into."

He got out to asses the predicament. He sank up to his ankles in the mud. The two men went to work trying to get the truck out. Nicole noted that although neither spoke they worked well together. All Wes needed to do was stretch out his hand and Richard handed him whatever it was that he needed. Both were irritated at the other but both understood what would be required before they could go home.

First they would dig a trench behind and under the back half of each wheel. This they lined with rocks, brush gravel or anything that was dry. While they pushed, Nicole would put the truck in reverse and try to back out. Each time it would move about three feet then drop off the dry bridge back into the mud. Then the process would be repeated. It appeared that dry ground was only thirty yards away. Already the men were beginning to tire and they had moved the pickup no more that eight feet.

"I need to go to the bathroom," Nicole announced desperately.

"There's some bushes at the edge of the bog," Wes gestured hardly looking up.

Nicole looked apprehensively at the slimy, smelly ooze.

"Here I'll give you a ride," Richard offered.

"Climb back into the bed."

Nicole did as she was told, then she climbed onto Richard's back from the tailgate. It was a terrible strain on him to lift his feet out of the sticky, sucking mud with each step.

"Hurry!" Nicole urged.

"Why didn't you tell me before?"

"I didn't want to be a nuisance. Don't jounce me."

"Don't get picky. I'm doing the best I can," Richard panted.

"I was only thinking of you," Nicole shot back. Richard surprised himself as the significance of the statement hit home. His legs came up higher and his speed increased but it only lasted for a few staggering steps. Thinking that it might be easier in the tracks made by the pickup Richard veered into the rut. It was easier and once again his speed increased but the footing was slicker and more treacherous. His feet shot to the side and they went down in a heap in the slime. They were only a few feet from dry ground. Nicole rolled off and sat next him.

"You are dirty now," Richard gasped. "You may as well walk out on your own."

"It's too late."

"Too late?"

"I'm sorry, I tried really hard not to but when we fell, the jar..." Nicole let her voice trail off when his horrified expression revealed he understood. His arm went around back to check the unbelievable. Several more hours of backbreaking work finally brought the truck on to dry ground. The mud splattered trio sank down in the dark to rest. The cool night wind felt wonderful as it dried their sweat soaked bodies.

"Some day we will look back on this adventure and laugh," Nicole predicted.

The absolute silence that met this statement led her to believe that that time was still in the distant future.

"Phew, Richard. What in the devil did you fall in?" Wes was sitting down wind. "Ride in back. I'll stop at the pond and let you bath before we go home."

Nicole ducked her head. "I'll ride in back with him."

Both Richard and Nicole plunged into the cool waters of the pond fully clothed except for shoes and belts and such. Richard removed his shirt and thoroughly rinsed it. Nicole moved away from him into deeper water. When the water was up to her neck she did the same.

"Wes come and hang these up for me," Richard called out. Nicole saw Wes hang up all Richard's clothes on a bush but his underwear. A moment later she handed her clothes to Richard to hand to Wes. She stayed in the deep water. She scrubbed herself until she felt clean and fresh; even her hair was free of mud. She felt a presence behind her.

"Richard! You stay away," She tried to swim away but he caught her by her bare leg and pulled her back. She found herself held tightly in his arms. He kissed her and ran his hands up her naked torso to her bra strap.

"Richard!" she protested weakly.

"Kinda like that don't you?"

Nicole didn't deny it. He kissed her again.

"Hey Dicky," Wes' voice boomed out over the water. "Git your butt outta there. Mrs. Defoe will be worried sick about us by now."

Richard tried to kiss her again.

"We better go." Nicole pulled away.

Their clothes were still damp but the wind streaming through the window began to dry them. The temperature began to drop as it will do in the desert at night. Nicole shivered. Richard put his arm around her. She snuggled up and laid her head on his shoulder. The events of the day began running through her mind much to her embarrassment.

"Richard, will you ever forgive me for what I did today?"

"I'll get over it," He recognized that at the moment she was vulnerable. He bent and kissed her.

"Uhummm." Wes cleared his throat.

"Wes, Mind your business!" Richard told him.

"If it is not my business then keep it to yourselves. That kinda thing can be kinda sickening on an empty stomach."

Nicole settled her head on Richard's shoulder and let the steady hum of the pickup put her to sleep.

On a regular basis for the next -few weeks, Wes and Richard visited the ranch. Wes gave the manager suggestions which were readily accepted. Whenever this happened the ranch hands always looked amused as if they knew something that she didn't. She determined to find out what was going on.

"Tell me something." She had followed Von into the barn and trapped him in a stall. Von was seventeen and fancied himself to be a real cowboy. Nicole figured he had a crush on her. He swaggered for her but seldom found anything to say.

"Do the guys like Wes?"

"Sure. Wes is a nice guy."

"Then why, when he makes suggestions, do they always smile like they are making fun of him?"

"They ain't making fun," Von smiled that

same mysterious smile.

"What are they laughing at then?"

"Cain't rightly say," Von evaded.

"Doesn't it strike you as odd that your boss would let Wes come in and tell him what to do?"

"No," Von was a poor liar.

"Your boss was very jealous of his position until Wes came," Nicole pointed out. "Is he thinking of leaving?"

"No, not that I know of."

Nicole put her hand on her hip tilted her head in a mildly coquettish manner. She looked Von directly in the eyes through her lowered lashes.

"Von," her voice took on a husky tone, "there are things that we could keep to ourselves. I hate to think you are leaving me out." With an effort Von managed to keep his cool.

"The boss and Wes made an agreement." Von disclosed.

"That is very interesting but it doesn't tell me much."

"Wes wanted the boss to pretend to take his advise."

"Why? What was Wes going to do for the boss?"

"It seems as though Wes is sweet on old Gabby, ah... excuse me, on Mrs. Defoe. He wanted to look good for her, ya know, act like the big man telling everyone what to do. He said Mrs. Defoe was sweet on him too. He was gonna put a good word in for the boss, build him up in her eyes, make him look good too. They actually sit down and plan out what they are going to say in front of Mrs. Defoe so that she can see the boss taking Wes' advice."

"They let the hired help listen in?"

"Sure. Wes wanted everyone to know that the boss still had the authority."

"This job must be pretty important to your boss."

"He loves this place. He grew up working here, but until Wes showed up, he was thinking of leaving. He don't like old...Mrs. Defoe."

"Mother isn't at all affectionate towards Wes. Why do the guys think she is sweet on him?"

"Wes says that she, being a foreigner has some strange ideas. He says the high toned and sophisticated don't believe in any show of feelings in front of the hired help."

"Von, you are a man of discretion. I won't breathe a word of this to anyone. Thank you very much. I would like to learn to ride better. Do you think you could take me to work with you?"

"I'd have to ask the boss," Von said uncertainly.

"Of course, maybe some other time,' Nicole made sure that Von felt that his lack of decisiveness was the reason for her not going.

So Wes was courting her mother. He was mighty slow about it; his manner toward her was always that of a helpful neighbor. Nicole had to admit that she had never known Wes to show anything but polite respect to any woman. He was almost backward. This coupled with the fact that her mother was recently widowed must explain their relationship.

As Nicole left town on her way home from work she noticed Wes's pickup parked near an older home surrounded by trees that sat back some distance from the road. She thought she recognized one of two figures on the porch roof as Richard. She shifted down and turned in. Richard climbed down and came over to greet her.

"What are you doing?" She asked.

"Putting on new shingles for old man Gothum."

"You surprise me. I didn't know you did this kind of work."

"I don't normally. Wes used to do carpentry work all the time when he needed extra money but they passed a new ordinance adopting the uniform building code. Wes says that with the licensing, insurance, both liability and workmen's compensation, and the bonding required, there isn't enough business to pay his expenses."

"So what are you doing here?"

"Charity case, some of the men came to Wes and asked him to help out. Gothum hasn't got the money and he is too proud to ask for help. Wes came over and acted like he was desperate for a stock trailer to move his cattle. He worked out a trade with Gothum, the use of the trailer for a week for a new roof on Gothum's porch. Wes will have to put some tires on the trailer before he can even move it."

"So, Gothum gets new tires too. That's mighty generous of you two.

"Wes is doing it mostly."

"Nonsense you're here too."

Another pickup drove up and parked next to Nicole. This one was an expensive four wheel drive.

"Are you working here?" A big officious looking man asked Richard the moment he stepped down from the vehicle. Richard pointed to Wes. The man walked away toward the house.

"Wes told me not to say a word to anybody I didn't know," Richard explained.

"Well, hello Wesly, what a surprise," He didn't sound the least bit surprised.

"Magelby," Wes acknowledged.

"Still at it I see," Wes didn't answer. "Must pay pretty well."

"Nope, no pay on this Job."

"Oh yes there is!" Old Gothum had just come out of the house. "That trailer over there is the pay. I don't live off other folk."

Magelby, smiling with great satisfaction, drew a pad from his pocket.

"Your name sir?" he spoke to Gothum.

"Harold Gothum," He answered with pride.

"Pleased to make your acquaintance," Magelby was busy writing.

"And here is your citation for hiring a man without a contractors license."

In the meant time, Wes had climbed down the ladder from the roof and was approaching.

"And Wesly, here is your citation for working without a contractor's license," With a flourish Magelby tore a sheet off the pad and handed it to Wes.

Without looking at it, Wes calmly tore it into quarters and with a grimy tar stained hand he stuffed it into Magelby's breast pocket leaving several black streaks on his white shirt. Wes continued to advance upon the surprised man. Magelby turned and scuttled away. Wes didn't follow but stood with a look of scorn on his face. With red angry face, the big man marched passed Richard and Nicole without a glance and jumped in his pickup and backed violently around and sped away.

"Richard!" Wes shouted, "We'll have to work like hell if we're gonna finish this job!"

Nicole sat nervously fingering her handbag that held a subpoena to appear in court as a witness in the case Wesly vs. the State of Nevada. The defendant was charged with operating a business without a contractor's license. She had come early to the court room to watch the proceedings concerning Harold Gothum's case. Gothum, byway of his counsel, pleaded guilty and was sentenced to ninety days in jail or upon payment of a three thousand dollar fine the jail sentence would be suspended.

"Mr. Gothum you are free to go. Your fine

has been paid," this from the same judge that had tried Wes' other case.

"Who paid it?" Gothum demanded.

"An anonymous donor, next case."

The prosecution for the state, once the preliminaries were out of the way, made his opening remarks to the jury that Wes once again had demanded.

"Your Honor, ladies and gentlemen of the jury, the state will show in this case that the defendant, Lionel Wesly, did willfully and knowingly violate the Uniform Building Code adopted by the State of Nevada, that he did threaten a state building inspector, that he did continue to work even after having been cited for illegal activities, that he did deceive with the intent to commit fraud."

"Your Honor, ladies and gentlemen of the jury, I intend to demonstrate without a doubt that the Uniform Building Code is contrary to the Constitution of the United States, not to mention the Constitution of the State of Nevada, and that the position of state building inspector is an illegal office and without authority to issue citations nor interfere with the labors of private citizens," These were Wes' opening remarks.

The prosecution called Richard Wesly as its first witness.

"Mr. Wesley, on the day that Inspector Magelby cited the defendant were you present?"

"I was."

"Did you see the defendant working on Mr. Gothum's roof?"

"I did."

"Did you in fact see the defendant receive a citation?"

"No sir."

"Come now Mr. Wesley, you were only a few yards away. I'm sure you were interested in what was happening. Surely you must have seen the inspector hand something to the defendant."

"I did."

"So which is it Mr. Wesley, did you or did you not see the inspector hand a citation to the defendant?"

"I had no idea what he handed to Wes."

"Did you help the defendant on the roof?"

"I did."

"Did the defendant have liability insurance to protect against possible lawsuits?"

"I don't know."

"Was the defendant thinking of with holding Social Security from your pay, or was he thinking he would just let you take your chances with the law in each of these cases?"

"No one can know how Wes thinks. Anyone in the valley can tell you that."

A good long chuckle accompanied by nodding heads showed general agreement to Richard's statement. The prosecution had no more questions. Wes did not cross examine.

"Mr. Magelby, tell the court what position you occupy."

"I am chief building inspector for the State of Nevada."

"Did you or did you not issue a citation to Lionel Wesly?"

"I did."

"Please tell the court what he did with it?"

"He tore it up and stuffed it in my pocket."

"What did he do then?"

"He threatened me."

"What did you do?"

"I went and obtained a warrant for his arrest and returned with several deputies. Mr. Wesley was still working on the roof."

The prosecution had no more questions. Wes arose to cross examine.

"Mr. Magelby, how is it that you were at Mr. Gothum's at that precise time?"

"I happened to be driving by on business and saw work being done in relation to my responsibilities. Naturally I stopped by to check it out."

"Naturally, no further questions."

Nicole was called as the next witness for the prosecution.

"Miss Defoe, did you see Mr. Wesly working on the roof?"

"Yes."

"Did you hear what was said?"

"Yes."

"Mr. Magelby has testified that the defendant threatened him. Would you describe what took place?"

"Wes scowled at him."

"Is that all?"

"Yes, then Magelby turned and ran."

Nicole's testimony was greeted with chuckles. The prosecution quickly abandoned questioning the witness.

"Nicole," Wes asked her, "you testified that you heard what was said?"

"Yes."

"Did you hear the inspector ask me if I had a license?"

"No."

"Did he ask to see my license?"

"No."

Wes asked no further questions. The prosecution called as witness a deputy sheriff.

"Were you present the night that the defendant was arrested?"

"I was."

"Please tell the court what happened."

"The Weslys were still on the roof working when we walked up. We ordered them to stop work and come down."

"Did they comply?"

"No. We thought that they were going to when Wes walked over to the ladder, but instead of coming down he pulled the ladder up."

"What did you do then?"

"We could see they were nearly done so we waited."

"So the defendant made several men sit and wait while he completed an illegal job?"

"That is correct."

Wes began the cross-examination.

"Tell me officer, did you threaten to shoot me if I didn't come down?"

"We did," The officer acted embarrassed by this question.

"Why didn't you?"

"It was an idle threat. We knew you weren't going anywhere. We decided to wait you out."

"Isn't it true you didn't shoot me because you knew it was wrong to kill me over a misguided law?"

"Objection your Honor."

"Sustained."

"Officer, is it still required of a police officer to take an oath by which he swears to uphold the constitution of the United States?

"Yes."

"Have you ever read this constitution?"

"We had a chapter on it in high school."

"Have you ever read it?"

"I've heard it discussed all my life"

"Have you ever read it?"

"No."

"As a police officer in the State of Nevada, did you take an oath to uphold the constitution of the state?

"I did."

"Have you ever read the state constitution?"

"No."

"Have you ever seen a copy of it in print?"

"No."

"When you arrested me for doing an honest day's work, were you upholding the constitution of the United States, and that of the State of Nevada or were you violating your oath?"

"Objection your Honor."

"On what grounds, counselor?"

"This man is sworn to uphold the law, not interpret it."

"That is my point, your honor," Wes defended, "how can this man uphold the law if he is completely ignorant of it as this man has demonstrated that he is?"

"Your honor, the purpose of this trial is not to discover the degree of understanding of this deputy but to show the guilt or innocence of the defendant," prosecution argued.

"Objection sustained."

Wes had no more questions for the witness. Mr. Harold Gothum was called to the stand as a witness for the prosecution.

"Mr. Gothum, would you tell the court how the defendant came to be working on your roof."

"He came to me explaining that he had heard that I wanted my roof fixed. He offered to do it for certain considerations."

"So you did hire him?"

"Yes."

"Did he tell you he had a license to perform such work?"

"No. I'd seen him do such work in the past. I naturally assumed that he was qualified."

"Or in other words, the defendant deceived you by not telling you anything.

"I must assume so."

Wes did not cross examine the witness. At this point the prosecution summarized its case.

"Your Honor, ladies and gentlemen of the jury, it has been clearly shown by the mouth of several witnesses that the defendant did willfully and knowingly engage in an illegal activity. It has been clearly shown that he did so under false pretenses. It has been clearly shown that once he had been discovered by the authorities that he, with an attitude of disdain for officers of the law, did continue until the job was completed. Although the defendant has pleaded innocent, he has yet to deny that he did the work or the charge that he did so without a license. The only reasonable verdict must be guilty as charged."

Wes began to call the witnesses for the defense.

"Mr. Barsee, do you live here in the valley?"

"I do."

"Have I ever done work for you?"

"You have."

"Will you tell the court what it is that I did for you?"

"You roofed my house."

"When was that?"

"About, five, six years ago.

"Are you happy with the work?"

"Yes."

"Mr. Avalon, have I ever done work for you?" Wes asked the second witness.

"Yes, Eight years ago. It was a roof job and it hasn't leaked a minute."

"Objection, your honor." The prosecution stated.

"Sustained, the witness will answer only the questions put to him," the judge instructed.

Wes called a third witness.

"Mr. Anderson, have I ever done work for you?"

"Yes."

"Objection, your honor, it is obvious that the defendant is trying to establish that he is a competent workman but that is not the issue. The issue is 'did he or did he not violate the law?'"

"Sustained," the Judge ruled.

"Did it leak?" Wes asked.

"Mr. Wesly, one more comment in defiance of the court and I will find you in contempt. Is that clear?"

"Yes, your honor."

"It didn't," Anderson answered the

question.

"Mr. Anderson, that goes for you too!" The Judge banged his gavel for emphasis.

Wes had no more questions for the witness. He called a fourth witness.

"Mr. Haliday, where do you live?"

"Kansas City."

"What do you do for a living?"

"I drive a truck."

"Have you ever been in the building trades?"

"Yes."

"Tell the court the procedure followed to satisfy a building inspector."

"As each phase of the building is finished, the inspector must be called. His okay is needed to continue."

"Mr. Haliday have you ever seen the structure changed after the inspector has finished?"

"Yes."

"Would you give an example to the court?"

"I've seen a wall built with bowed two-by-fours that were cut nearly through after the inspector left."

"What was the purpose of this?"

"The wall could be pushed straight and the sheet rock would hold it in place."

"Could you give us a second example?"

"I saw re-bar laid and fastened in place for cement to be poured over it in footings. As soon as the inspector was gone, the re-bar was jerked up and laid in the next section. A short piece of re-bar was left in at the joint so that the next time the inspector came he would see it sticking out of the hardened cement."

"This was to lead him to believe that all the footings had re-bar, is that correct?"

"Yes."

"Thank you Mr. Haliday. I would like to call Hal Green to the stand please."

"Now Mr. Green," Wes continued once the witness was sworn in, "did you ever work with Mr. Haliday in construction?"

"Your Honor," the prosecution interrupted

"I must object. I can see no connection between this line of questioning and the issue before the court."

"Mr. Wesly," the judge instructed, "you must show the relevance of the line of questioning or abandon it."

"It is very relevant to my case," Wes assured him. The judge looked skeptical but allowed him to continue.

"While you were working with Mr. Haliday did you witness these two examples that he has described?"

"I did."

"Did you participate?"

"We helped on the wall but refused to pour the footings without re-bar."

"What happened as a result of your refusal?"

"We were fired."

"How many were fired?"

"Three."

"Who was the third?"

"You Wes."

"Tell the court what our former employer does for a living."

"He is chief building inspector for the State of Nevada."

"Objection, Your Honor! The defendant is not seeking the facts to show his innocence but is trying to distract the jury with sensational but irrelevant testimony. He is trying to excuse himself by pointing out the faults of others but this trial is for the purpose of determining HIS guilt or innocence!"

"Objection sustained."

Nicole could plainly see that Wes had succeeded in irritating the judge, jury and prosecuting attorney. Many of the spectators were irritated also but a few were enjoying the spectacle. She decided it was entertaining to watch Wes' thrashing about, but the outcome was a foregone conclusion. Wes succeeded in recalling Mr. Magelby to the stand.

"Mr. Magelby, you testified that you were just passing by when you stopped and gave me a citation, is that correct?"

"Yes, yes, it is."

"Isn't it true that you received a call from this valley informing you of my activities, and isn't it true that you took the opportunity to take revenge upon me for having exposed your corrupt business practices from times past?"

"Objection your Honor. The defendant is pursuing the same line of questioning."

"Sustained."

"Your Honor, I intend to prove that this witness is a damned liar! His testimony shouldn't be allowed."

"Mr. Wesly, there will be no name calling in this courtroom," the judge reprimanded him.

"The man has committed perjury and I can prove it. I ask that the court allow me to continue."

"Very well Mr. Wesly, but make sure you don't mock this court."

"Thank you. Mr. Magelby did you or did you not come to this valley because of an informer?"

"I did not."

"No further questions. I would like to call Bonnie Masters to the stand."

With a feeling of hope growing in her, Nicole watched Magelby's face pale at the sound of this name.

"Miss Masters, tell the court where you work."

"I work at the state capital in Mr. Magelby's office."

"In the course of your work some

information dealing with this case came into your hands. Is that correct?"

"Yes."

"Would you please enlighten the court?"

"I was instructed to disperse a check to the citizen that turned you in Mr. Wesly."

"Under whose instructions did you do this?"

"Mr. Magelby's."

A murmur ran through the court room.

"Is the citizen that received the reward in the court room today?"

"He is."

"And what is his name?"

"I'm not allowed to tell. By law this information is confidential."

"Is he sitting on the jury?"

"Objection, Your honor! This law is set up to protect those who try to help reduce crime. They shouldn't be subjected to persecution even by association. This court is subject to and set up to enforce the law."

The counsel for the prosecution was too late. Nicole and many others had seen Bonnie begin to nod her head in the affirmative before she was interrupted.

"Sustained," the judge ruled.

"Because of the shadow of suspicion that has fallen upon the proceedings of this court I ask that a mistrial be declared," Wes petitioned the court.

The judge called for an adjournment to take

the matter under advisement.

Chapter 5

It was amazing to Nicole how well prepared Wes had come to this trial. How on earth had he learned of this supposedly confidential information? The opportunity to find out was not long in coming, for she found herself waiting in the hall with Bonnie. She introduced herself as Richard's girlfriend, hoping to gain Bonnie's confidence. Bonnie was carefully groomed, slender and gave the impression of being wealthy but beneath the surface elegance she was rather plain and unsure.

"Richard?"

"Richard Wesly, Wes'... "

"Oh, yes, from the other family."

"Do you know Wes well?"

"No. I never set eyes on him before today. I talked briefly with him on the phone a while back."

"That was brave of you to testify for him. Will it affect your job do you think?"

"It doesn't matter. Sophi has promised me a job."

"Sophi?" Nicole prompted.

"Yes , I'm close friends with Sophi."

"Who is Sophi?"

Bonnie suddenly eyed her with suspicion. She clamed up and refused to answer any more questions. Wes at that moment came down the hall from the judge's chambers.

"Sophi wanted me to convey her love,"

Bonnie told him awkwardly.

"And I wish to send her mine. Thank her for her help, and thank you too Bonnie. I'll be forever in your debt."

Bonnie glowed from his praise. She excused herself and left. Nicole had wanted to encourage Wes in his efforts but Richard needed to be on his way so she allowed him to take her home without speaking to Wes.

"Who is Sophi?" she asked once they were on the way.

"Wes' ex."

"Another one?"

Richard laughed at Nicole's tone of voice.

"Wes has an eye for classy little women but he doesn't understand the first thing about them."

"She is pretty then?"

"No, she's not pretty..... she is beautiful, a real fox." Richard had a faraway look in his eye as he remembered her image.

"Hey!" Nicole chided him.

"Not to worry," Richard grinned at her, "she is ten years older than I."

The trial resumed the following day. Wes' appeal for a mistrial was denied on the grounds that a citizen that was doing his duty as a citizen should not be denied the right to serve on jury duty and that doing one's duty in one area did not prove prejudice in another. The name of the juror in question was not revealed.

"Your Honor," Wes continued his defense,

"I would like to make a statement before the court." He was sworn in as a witness.

"I do testify before the court that I, Lionel Wesly, do, by the laws of this state and the laws of this country, have the right to work in any honest labor that I desire and that my rights as a sovereign citizen have been violated by the officers of this county and by officials of the state of Nevada." Wes finished his statement then stepped down.

"In view of the fact that Mr. Wesly was on the stand as a witness, the prosecution asks the right to cross-examine."

"Please return to the stand Mr. Wesly," The judge instructed. "You are still under oath."

"Mr. Wesly do you or do you not have a license to conduct business in the building trades in this county?"

"I do."

"You do?" Counsel for the prosecution was at a loss for a moment but quickly recovered.

"The records from the state that I have here show you don't have one. If you don't have a license issued by the state from whom have you received your license?" Counsel was now sure of his ground.

"From God."

"Oh, from God. I would be curious to see it." This was said with sarcastic mirth. He was joined by a ripple of laughter from the spectators.

"I have the documents right here on the

desk." Wes got the needed papers and returned to the stand. "I would like to enter these documents as evidence." The judge briefly examined the papers then handed them to the prosecution.

"Your honor, I object."

"On what grounds?"

The prosecution blinked his eyes in surprise.

"These documents are hardly applicable in this case."

"Not applicable?" The judge returned.

"I mean there is no connection. . ." he stammered then fell silent in confusion.

"May I explain to the jury?" Wes asked the judge.

"Proceed."

"I have just entered as evidence the Declaration of Independence, the Constitution of the United States and the Constitution of the State of Nevada as my license to work in particular may I quote briefly. 'We hold these truths to be self-evident that all men are created equal that they are endowed by their creator with certain inalienable rights, that among these are life, liberty, and the pursuit of happiness. That to secure these rights, governments are instituted among men, deriving their Just powers from the consent of the governed.' Of course you recognize this from the Declaration of Independence. This document was approved unanimously and signed by fifty-six prominent leaders of the revolution who sat as representatives of the several states. Let me now quote from the

Constitution where in it implements these ideas. 'WE the people of the United States'."

This quote clearly conveys the idea that sovereignty lies with the people. That government has only those powers that are delegated to it by the people. It also should be abundantly clear that the people can delegate to government only those powers that they themselves possess, which are the right to protect their life, liberty, and property in word and deed. The first two amendments, found in the Bill of Rights, guarantees these rights, the right to freedom of speech and the right to keep and bear arms. Anything more is usurpation and anything less is dereliction of duty."

"Your honor," the prosecution interrupted, "this is an interesting political theory but it has little to do with the present case. The defendant is being tried for breaking a state law."

"Mr. Wesly you may continue if you can quickly show how to apply these laws to your specific case." The Judge was interested.

"Yes, Your honor. In order to do this I would call one more witness, Mr. Orval Redding."

Mr. Redding was sworn in.

"Mr. Redding, tell the court what you do for a living."

"I am Attorney General for the State of Nevada."

"What are your duties in this capacity?"

"I am the head of the Justice Department. I am responsible for the prosecution of criminals in the state."

"Have you ever read and studied the Constitution of the United States?"

"I have."

"Have you ever read and studied the Constitution of the state of Nevada?"

"I have."

"Is it true that the Federal constitution requires each State to have a Republican form of government that secures the rights of the people as outlined in the federal Constitution?"

"It does."

"Therefore we can assume that the Constitution of this State complies with this criteria?"

"We can."

"Mr. Redding, do you own a home?"

"I do."

"How did you acquire this home? Did you steal it?"

"Objection, your Honor. The witness is not on trial here," The prosecution argued.

"Sustained."

"May the witness describe how he came by his home? It is not my intention to accuse the witness in any manner."

"The witness may answer this question." The Judge ruled.

"I bought it."

"On contract?"

"Yes."

"If you had defaulted on your contract, what recourse would be open to the seller?"

"He could take me to court and repossess the house."

"Does the government have the authority to do that?"

"It does."

"On what grounds?"

"The state has the right to protect the property of the seller. The Constitution states clearly that government has the right to enforce contracts."

"That is a nice suit you are wearing. How did you acquire it?"

"I bought it."

"Do you drive a nice car?"

"I do."

"How did you acquire it?"

"I bought it."

"Does your wife have a nice car?"

"Your honor, there is no point to this line of questioning," The prosecution protested.

"Make your point, Mr. Wesly."

"Yes, your Honor. Mr. Redding have you ever acquired anything that you did not work for?"

"I have received some by inheritance."

"Is there any other legal way of acquiring property?"

"There is one other way. Through government programs designed to assist the poor and the needy."

"What would happen to me if I decided I was poor and needed a car to go to work so I went over to my neighbor's house and simply drove off in his?"

"You would be arrested and brought to trial for theft."

"If I as a citizen do not have the right to seize my neighbor's property, how can I delegate that right to my government? May I point out that the confiscation of goods by government for redistribution is socialism and is abhorrent to every patriotic American. If one does not inherit property then the only way that he can acquire it is through his labor as pointed out by our Attorney General. Therefore, to limit a man in his right to work infringes one's right to property. To the extent that one is limited in his property by government he is limited in his liberty, and deprived of all property both real and personal he suffers death.

The documents upon which our nation and state are founded clearly state that the right to work comes from God not the state. It is upon this premise that dictates that the uniform building code is contrary to the laws of God and the laws of the land.

Mr. Redding, you say that you are familiar with the constitutions of both state and federal government. Can you point out any amendment that has negated the rights I have described?"

"No, however…"

"Then you must agree that the law under

which I am accused is null and void."

"Objection, Your Honor! The defense is calling for an opinion of the witness, furthermore, it is not the right of the attorney general to interpret the law nor to declare the constitutionality of a law."

"Sustained."

"Mr. Redding, did you take an oath of office declaring that you would uphold the Constitution of the United States and that of the State of Nevada?"

"I did."

"Thank you, no more questions."

"Mr. Redding," the prosecution began "did the state legislature adopt the uniform building code as law in the State of Nevada?"

"It did."

"And is it in force until such time as it is declared unconstitutional?"

"It is."

"Is it the prerogative of this court to declare that the law is unconstitutional?"

"No it is not."

"Thank you, no further questions."

Both sides were finished with the witnesses. Court was adjourned until the following day. The prosecution's final arguments would be heard first thing in the morning.

Nicole, Richard and Wes sat in the cafe over supper. Nicole and Richard were quiet and subdued, feeling that it would be the last for many days with Wes. Wes was the same as always, laughing and talking and generally enjoying himself but he too finally became quiet in the face of so little response. There was little to break the silence but the soft clink of utensils on china. Two men the entered the cafe and sat in the next booth.

"How do you think it will turn out?" one asked.

"He has about as much chance as a snowball in hell."

"I thought he made some good points today."

"Irrelevant. He is a damned trouble maker and thinks he is above the law. It don't pay to be such an eccentric."

"I guess he is kinda arrogant but…"

"No buts about it. He's been up before. They'll send him up again."

"Still …"

"Forget it. Let's talk about something pleasant while we eat. It's better for your digestion, I've heard."

Wes looked at Richard but he was concentrating on his food. His eyes shifted and looked into Nicole's. She too dropped her eyes to her plate. The men were right, she felt, he didn't stand a chance.

The closing arguments of the prosecution were short and precise.

"The testimony of several witnesses has clearly shown that the defendant did willfully and knowingly break the law. He was belligerent at the time of his arrest. The defendant himself could not show a license recognized by the state. He never attempted to deny he did the illegal work. His conduct throughout the trial has demonstrated a rebellious and seditious attitude towards his government. His only defense has been to attempt to show the unconstitutionality of the law.

However, the head of the State Justice Department has testified that it is not the prerogative of this court to make such a decision. Your Honor, Ladies and Gentlemen of the jury, I submit that the defendant has been shown to be guilty of all charges without doubt," The prosecution finished.

Wes began.

"Your Honor, Ladies and Gentlemen of the jury. May I at this time demonstrate by the law the prerogatives of this court? John Jay, a patriot deeply involved in the constitutional debates and first Chief Justice of the Supreme Court, in the first case that was tried by jury before his court in Georgia vs. Brailsford had this to say; 'It may not be amiss here, gentlemen, to remind you of the good old rule that in questions of fact, it is the providence of the jury, on question's of law it is the providence of the court to decide. But it must be observed that by the same law, which recognizes this reasonable distribution of jurisdiction, you have nevertheless a right to take upon yourselves to judge of both, and to determine the law as well as the fact controversy. On this, and on every other occasion, however we have no doubt you will pay that respect which is due to the opinion of the court; for, as on the one hand, it is presumed that the jury are the best judges of the fact's, it is on the other hand, presumed that the courts are the best judges of the law. But still, both objects are lawfully within your power of decision.'

Let me quote Thomas Jefferson; 'In the case of a combination of law and fact, it is usual for the jurors to decide the fact, and to refer the law arising on it to the decision of the judges. But this division of the subject lies with the discretion of the jurors.'

I quote Theophilius Parsons, Chief Justice of the Supreme Court of Massachusetts; 'An act of usurpation is not obligatory; it is not law; and any man may be justified in his resistance. Let him be considered as a criminal by the general government, yet only his fellow citizens can convict him; they are his jury, and if they pronounce him innocent, not all the powers of Congress can hurt him, and innocent they certainly will pronounce him if the supposed law he resisted was an act of usurpation.'

"May I quote Lysander Spooner, another great American a statesman: 'For more than six hundred years - that is, since the Magna Carta, in 1215 — there has been no clearer principle of English or American constitution law , than that in criminal cases, that is not only the right and duty of the juries to judge what are the facts, what is the law, and what was the moral intent of the accused; but that it is also their right and paramount duty, to judge of the justice of the law, and to hold all laws invalid, that are, in their opinion, unjust or oppressive, and all persons guiltless in violating, or resisting the execution of, such laws.'

I have shown by the testimony of three witnesses that it is possible to do good quality, honest work without a license from the state. I have also shown by testimony that the possession of a license does not guarantee good quality or honest work. I have shown that the law creates another agency that is capable of doing great damage to the citizens through corrupt officials, whereas an individual citizen has the power to do only a small amount of damage and even then he is subject to the laws legitimately protecting life, liberty and property. Not only have I demonstrated that the law is a bad law but I have demonstrated that it is contrary to the federal constitution as well as the state constitution, that it is an usurpation of the state in an attempt to practice extortion by demanding that a citizen buy protection through insurance, that a citizen must pay a bondsman, that a citizen must pay the state a fee, that a citizen must pay those who cease to work through unemployment tax and income tax, that a citizen must in short, pay dearly for the God given right to work. All is done through the usurpation of power and illegal use of force. If the citizen does not comply he is fined and or incarcerated. Although it is not the right of this jury to repeal the law it is well within their right and it is their duty and obligation to find me innocent of all charges."

Wes was finished and sat down.

"He's right!' Nicole whispered. "They can't find him guilty now!'

The jury deliberated for three hours. It not being late in the day, court was declared once again to be in session.

"Your Honor, we find the defendant ...guilty of all charges," The jury foreman informed the court.

"Oh no!" Nicole groaned. "It went right over their heads!"

"He was grasping at straws," Richard opined.

"Will the accused please stand. You are hereby sentenced to pay a fine of three thousand dollars and ninety days in jail. The jail sentence will be commuted upon payment of the Fine."

"Your Honor, I decline to give the fruits of my labor to be used by the corrupt officials that have combined to persecute honest citizens."

"Your sentence will begin immediately."

"Your Honor," Wes spoke up, "I ask mercy of court. May I begin the sentence after the holidays? I have a date for the New Years dance."

"Sentence will begin on January first without fail!" The judge was clearly irritated.

"Once again Richard and Nicole waited outside the judge's chambers for Wes. The door was closed this time but they could clearly hear the words coming from inside.

"Wes, I can't believe that you could so

completely miss the obvious. All you had to do was to call those men as witnesses that knew that the work you were doing was charity. Even if you had been convicted, I would have had grounds to be lenient."

"That's not the point."

"Not the point? Sometimes Wes, I think you enjoy making a fool of yourself. When are you going to quit being a knot head and hire a decent lawyer when you get in trouble?"

"There is a top notch lawyer that has agreed to represent me. He was here for the trial."

"Agreed to represent you? If you are thinking of appealing, you don't stand a chance in hell of winning unless you follow my advice and change your tactics."

"I'm not appealing. I'm going to sue you, Ben."

"Why? What have I done to you? I'm the best friend you'll ever have in this court! I've tried everything I know to help you, but you ignore me!"

"You have violated your oath of office. You all but told the jury that the Constitution was no longer in effect and that they were obligated to convict me because of the popular traditions of American jurisprudence since 1895."

"What on earth are you talking about?"

"Ben for all the learning that you have received over these many years you have not came to understand the truth but now you will have to study what you should have known before you ever took your oath of office."

"You are wasting your money. In fact I know you don't have the money."

"I don't need any money. My lawyer and five others are willing to keep you in court for a good many years at their own expense. If we never win, you will be bankrupt. You won't be sitting as judge."

"I'll counter sue. I'm not a poor man. I assure you no damned fringe group lawyer will ever know the law like I do," The Judge stated confidently.

"Ben, are you familiar with the name Harvey Stoneridge? How 'bout the name Fern Tendill?"

There was a deep silence in the judge's chambers.

"Why, Wes?" The judge's suddenly worried voice was barely discernible through the door.

"You are in an important position. You are doing a lot of damage because you are a comfortable, complacent ignoramus."

"Damn you! I'll not stand for that!"

"Why not? You have been calling me a knot head for years. You've claimed to be my friend the whole time. Are you going to throw our friendship out the window the first time I return the favor? After all I'm doing all this for your own good."

"My own good?"

"Sure, if you could just see the obvious it would save everybody a lot of bother."

"What is obvious to you Wes is a total mystery to everybody else." The judge didn't mean this as a compliment.

"I'm thinking that you should forget this jurisprudence tradition horse manure and study the real law, the Constitution, and fulfill your oath of office."

"I have the feeling I'm being blackmailed," The judge said with feeling.

Nicole had wanted to tell Wes that she had felt inspired by his impassioned plea for justice but as he emerged from the judge's chambers he was immediately joined by two men she had never seen before.

"You did a good job," She managed to say as he went by.

"Thank you, sweetheart," He continued down the hall with his companions without stopping.

Chapter 6

The Weslys arrived at the Defoe home on New Years Eve all dressed for the dance. Nicole had maneuvered for several weeks to get Wes to invite her mother. This was the first date her mother had accepted since her father had died. The men helped the ladies on with their wraps and led them into the cold night to the truck. The moon was bright on the skiff of snow that had fallen the previous night making the desert resemble the ocean, except the waves were stationary. Their breath rose in clouds from the twenty degree weather. Sitting in the cab of the truck with two big men made the fit quite snug. Richard put his arm around Nicole and Nicole put her arm around her mother.

To start out Wes put the gear shift toward him and back. Second gear was forward and to the right but when he was ready to shift straight back into third he found a pair of knees in the way.

"Uhumm." He cleared his throat. He had shifted into neutral and the pickup began to lose speed.

"Ah,....Mrs. Defoe, you will have to spread your knees and let me shift back between them or you'll have to put your knees closer to me."

Nicole saw her mother's facial muscles tense but there was no other alternative. She moved closer to Wes. Nicole and Richard carried on an intermittent conversation but the other couple seemed to have lost their tongues.

"There's a coyote!" Wes exclaimed. The pickup immediately began to slow.

"Wes, not tonight!" Richard protested.

"This will only take a minute," Wes assured him. The pickup drifted to a quiet stop and Wes got out. He reached for his rifle in the sling In front of the seat.

"Richard, what have you done with my rifle?"

"Wes, we're on our way to a dance not on a hunting trip," Richard argued reasonably.

"You leave my things alone, Dicky," Wes put a distinct accent on the last word. The rest of the trip was made in silence. All the people in the valley were there, young and old. The band was in full swing and they were good, playing a wide variety of music, everything from soft rock to old fashioned waltzes, but they specialized in country swing. Richard had taken Nicole dancing before and had taught her to dance country swing which she now preferred. On the first waltz he pulled her close and they glided around the floor as one. He was an excellent dancer with a smooth graceful rhythm.

Nicole was having a good time but Richard was still mad.

"What is this thing Wes has against coyotes?" She encouraged him to talk it out.

"They kill his lambs and calves."

"Do all the ranchers hate the coyote?"

"Sure, but they are reasonable men, not fanatics like Wes. Let's not talk about Wes."

"Let's not think about him either then and have some fun," Nicole chided him.

"Done," Richard smiled and whirled her about the floor.

Nicole got a glimpse of her mother and Wes on the floor but didn't see them again for some time. After dancing steadily for thirty minutes Nicole took a break and went to the powder roam. She returned to find Richard dancing with Amy with Amy's date standing on the side lines looking on. Linda managed to dance with Richard a couple of times but Amy was too persistent and aggressive for her and she gave up. Meanwhile, Nicole's mother was dancing with the ranch manager and seemed to be having a good time. The middle aged men discovered her mother and she was kept on the dance floor. Wes sat by himself in the shadows. Feeling responsible because she had basically arranged the date for him Nicole went to keep him company.

They sat in silence for the music was too loud to allow conversation. Amy continued to dominate Richard's time.

"Would you care to dance?" Nicole finally asked.

"Yes, it is a nice dance," Wes answered.

"I said...." Nicole realized she was almost

shouting. She took him by the hand and pulled him onto the dance floor. With the same grace and rhythm as Richard but with more energy and flair, Wes spun her around the floor. Rather than dancing the swing' like everyone else, Wes had taken her in his arms and began an old fashioned but simple step. With long easy strides he guided her expertly among the dancers. They traveled swiftly, around the floor as if Wes thought that the object of dancing was to get someplace. It was amazing to her how Wes could avoid the closely packed dancers, yet whirl her first in one direction then another.

She began to let herself relax and really have a good time.

"Sorry," Wes apologized. He had tromped her toe hard. Some of the flair went out of his dancing as he tried to be more cautious but along with the flair went some of his rhythm.

"Sorry," He was apologizing again shortly thereafter. His dancing now was now quite stilted and mechanical.

"Sorry," Wes stopped and leaned closer. I think you better rescue Richard if you want to dance with him again tonight. With this Wes excused himself and returned to the side lines.

"Thanks, honey, Richard smiled ruefully; I didn't know how I was going to get rid of her short of being rude."

The return trip was pleasant. A flush of excitement was still on her mother's face. Nearly every man over the age of thirty five had asked her to dance. She talked enthusiastically about the next dance being planned for Valentine's Day. Wes was a good sport agreeing that it had been a nice evening even though he had hardly danced at all. Nicole guessed that her mother's toes were as sore as her own. She rested her head on Richard's shoulder and was content to listen. Life took a definite turn for the worse in Nicole's opinion. Richard returned to Reno to attend school for the winter quarter and Wes went to Jail.

The accountant that had been handling their finances reported that the ranch expenses had decreased significantly and their income had increased a little. Her mother announced that it would now be possible for Nicole to return to school. Strange as it seemed even to herself, Nicole felt a real reluctance to leave. First there was the pressure of arranging everything on short notice. It would be unfair to Mr. Trimble to quit without notice.

Her desire to work as an interior decorator had diminished. She didn't want to give up her rides over the desert with Von. Finally she admitted to herself that the valley that she had so hated at first had seduced her. She didn't want to live anywhere else. Even the thought of being in the same city as Richard was not enough to spur her to action. The winter quarter began without her.

Out of a vague sense of duty Nicole visited Wes once a week to start with, but for the lack of anything else to do she formed the habit of going by each day after work. The jailer got used to her and allowed her to sit in the same room with Wes. At first Wes had complained of the same problems that he had faced on the previous occasion but after a while he talked little. He lost weight again and began to look pale. Nicole tried to cheer him up but he began to tell morbid jokes that only depressed her. Wes would get up and pace and not talk to her. She didn't find the visits enjoyable but she was drawn back time and time again.

She knew that Wes cherished his freedom above all else but had chosen jail rather than compromise. Although he didn't do well at all in confinement a certain light never went out of his eyes. Shortly after Wes' releases Richard returned to the valley for spring vacation. The Weslys came to the ranch for the first time in months. Nicole listened as Wes once again began advising Roark, the ranch manager. He did so with less assurance and he almost had attitude of one advising a superior. She attributed this to the fact that her mother and Roark were on better terms. Roark had taken her mother to the Valentines dance while Wes was in jail. More and more her mother had relied on him as the prosperity of the ranch improved. Nicole felt sorry for Wes. She realized that he had been supplanted as her mother's suitor.

"Well Richard we better go check on the condition of the spring range."

Wes had withdrawn quickly from the planning session. He must have decided that his cause was lost. Richard had invited Nicole to go with them. Their trip began in the same direction as the year before but once or the high desert, as the mesa was called, they turned north instead of south. After many miles, Wes pulled to a stop atop a small rise overlooking a vast, flat plain where nothing grew but a few scattered sagebrush and these n more than eight inches in height.

"See this big bare spot?" he asked. "The old timers named it Bare Spot."

"Original," Richard snickered.

"Very creative," Nicole agreed. They laughed.

Wes looked insulted. He hadn't recovered his natural good humor after his stay in jail. His paleness had been replaced by a bad sunburn adding to his ill temper.

"There is a spring over by that ridge we should check out," Wes turned the pickup off the road and started across the flat. The ground was surprisingly smooth allowing them to travel at a good speed. Nicole could tell that Wes was familiar with area.

"There's a coyote!" Wes exclaimed.

The pickup was brought quickly to a stop. Wes stepped out and smoothly drew his rifle out and up.

"Sharp movements scare the critter," He instructed them. Simultaneously with the report of the rifle the coyote leaped into the air and raced across the flat.

"Damn, missed him!"

Wes jumped back into the truck.

"We'll wait here," Richard jumped out the other side and pulled on Nicole's hand.

"Richard!" she protested. "I'd rather not stand out in the hot sun."

"You will regret…"

"He's getting away!" With this statement Wes stomped on the gas, the truck leaped forward causing the door to slam shut leaving Richard coughing in the dust.

"Here, hold this," Wes shoved the rifle at her. She set the butt on the truck floor with the muzzle up. She concentrated on controlling the direction it was pointing. She didn't want to accidentally shoot anyone. The speed of the pickup worried her and she glanced down at the speedometer, she wished she hadn't, they were traveling over sixty miles an hour. As the tires vibrated over the scattered clumps of sage brush it felt like they were traveling over a washboard but they were gaining on the coyote. Once they were right on his tail, Wes slid the pickup to a stop and jerked the rifle from her and jumped out. Dust kicked up at the feet of the fleeing animal. It leaped into the air and came down turning at a right angle heading for the ridge.

"Can't let him on the ridge, can't follow him," Wes explained as he gunned the truck. Nicole could see that the animal was about to escape. Wes once more brought the truck to a stop and grabbed the rifle and leaped out. Dust kicked up just in front of the animal. This time the coyote turned a hundred and eighty degrees and raced back the way it had come and sped by. Wes missed again, this time by a wide margin. Several more times Wes repeated the procedure each time narrowly missing. Nicole had lost all sense of direction and they were miles from the starting point.

"Load this," Wes commanded after one more miss and he shoved the rifle back to her. "The shells are in the glove compartment."

"There are only four shells," Nicole reported
"Plenty."

Nicole managed to load the rifle and hold it ready. Suddenly out of nowhere, a wash twenty feet wide and about the same in depth appeared directly in front of them. A glance Nicole revealed that the speedometer was near seventy. She screamed. Wes, at the same instant, braked and then seeing it was too late put the gas feed to the floor and swerving slightly, brought the truck to a small rise on the near side of the wash. Nicole felt the vehicle leave the ground and soar through the air. The back wheels caught the lip of the wash on the far side, throwing the rear end abruptly back into the air. Two more hard bounces and the truck came to a stop. Nicole had banged her head three times on the roof. The rifle, desperately gripped by the stock, had followed her up and down smashing through the windshield on each trip.

"Are you alright, sweetheart?" Wes looked concerned.

"Yes, I'm fine," Nicole answered tentatively.

"The varmint is getting away!"

Four shots later the coyote was still untouched but staggering with fatigue. Wes pulled the truck alongside and leaping out, raced up to the still fleeing coyote and smashed it behind the ear with the butt of the rifle. The coyote rolled and came to its feet. Wes smashed it a second time killing it, but also breaking the stock off his rifle.

Richard, once they finally found him, eyed the broken windshield, the broken gun stock and the small cut on Nicole's hand with a knowing 'I told you so' smirk.

"The rim on the rear right is bent and the tire is leaking air," He informed them.

"No problem," Wes answered confidently.

"I've got a good spare," He jumped out and walked around back. They heard him curse.

"Dicky! Have you been using my Jack?"

Richard and Nicole both went to the back of the truck to check out this new disaster with their own eyes.

"The last time I saw your jack you were using it to fix the tire on your baler," Richard reminded him with satisfaction

"Oh, yeah, that's right," Wes mumbled.

"What will we do now?"

Nicole was thinking of the long walk home.

"Quick, get back in the pickup!"

The tire was low but could be driven for a short time longer. Wes raced back toward the road on the ridge. The terrain not being so flat, Wes found what he was looking for, a rock protruding from the ground. He quickly drove the leaking tire onto it and stopped. Setting the brake, he then turned.

"Quick, help me find something to use as a block."

Wes jumped out and shoved two boards from the back of the truck under the rear axle. Richard, seeing immediately what he was doing ran around and found some flat rocks and set these on top of the boards forming a nice steady block for the axle to rest on. No sooner were they in place than the truck settled slowly until it rested solidly into place. Wes pushed the valve stem to more quickly release the air, and then he loosened the lug nuts and with a little struggle removed the flat tire.

"There," He grinned triumphantly, "there is no cause for alarm with ol' Wes on the job."

Richard rolled the spare into place only to discover that with the tire fully inflated it sat too high to go on the lug bolts. He looked at Wes with accusing eyes.

"Good hell man!" Wes scoffed, "All we have to do now is dig around this rock and pull it out of the way."

The ground was only one degree softer than the rock. Wes chipped away at it for a while, and then Richard would take his turn. Wes began using the tire iron as a spade. This sped up the work but it was a long time before the men slid the rock out of the way. It was much larger than they had anticipated. The tire went on with room to spare but it was left spinning freely in the air.

"Now what?" Richard wanted to know.

"Didn't anyone ever teach you to think? We will fill up the hole."

"What good will that do? We can't pack the dirt tight enough under the wheel to get any traction,' Richard argued.

Wes looked disgusted.

"After we fill up the hole we get in the pickup and drive off the blocks. The other tire is solid on the ground and will have plenty of traction. This tire then will not fall in the hole. We'll drive right away, simple."

They scraped all the loose dirt into the hole but it didn't replace the space left by the rock. After shoveling in all the loose dirt within several yards, what had been the hole was a slight depression.

"That ought to do it," Wes declared. They climbed into the pickup and Wes put it in gear and let up on the clutch. The tire spun. Wes tried for several minutes to rock the truck off the blocks but without success. Richard nodded his head to show that he wasn't surprised.

"All we have to do now is dig around the blocks," Wes glared at him.

Wes crawled under the truck in front of the rear tire and dug with the tire iron. Richard dug from the rear with the shovel. The space was limited. The swing of the tools was short and awkward so the ground gave way with one small chip at a time as the time slipped slowly by.

"Trade me places," Wes demanded. "This is awful work for an old man."

He crawled out all sweaty and dirty. Richard crawled under the truck. The men were tired out and had to rest every few minutes.

"Let's give it a try," Richard suggested hopefully.

Wes started the truck and revved the motor. Wes popped the clutch and the pickup lurched forward but came to a stop with its tire spinning.

"Stop!" Richard screamed.

Wes put in the clutch as he let up on the gas.

"What's the matter?"

Richard pointed. Wes got out and walked around the truck. Much of the loose dirt had been thrown out of the hole and the tire wouldn't climb up over the hard lip of the hole.

"All we have to do now is finish getting the blocks out of the way and knock that lip off the hole so the tire can climb out on a nice gentle incline."

The blocks were fairly easy to remove but to remove the lip from the hole took more, painfully slow, digging. Of course the frame of the pickup was next to the ground over the hole, making it awkward to dig and limiting the space to one worker. Finally in a cloud of dust Wes managed to drive the pickup out of the hole.

"Get Nicole, it's time to head home," Wes directed.

Richard looked around but couldn't see her. He walked around behind the pickup and turned to the west. He shaded his eyes with his hand against the sun sitting just above the horizon and stared out at the huge expanse of the empty desert. Nothing moved. He walked quickly to the top of the ridge and anxiously scanned the empty desert to the east.

"She's gone, Wes!"

"Gone? Can't be, there is no place to go."

Wes got out and duplicated Richard's movements.

"See!" Richard looked nervously at the lowering sun.

"Hummm," Wes began walking in a circle thirty yards from the truck.

"She went that way," He stopped, his finger rising to point out her tracks leading off toward the north. "That's where the spring is."

95

Nicole was a vision of cool crisp loveliness sitting on the grass in the tiny grove of trees with her feet in the pool made by the spring. The two tired, dirty men sank to their knees and drank deeply from the source of the water.

"Am I glad to see you. I was getting a little nervous about getting out of here before dark, besides I'm hungry," Nicole pulled her feet out of the water. They climbed into the truck and turned eastward toward home Richard stretched his tired body and leaned back with a groan.

"Tired?" Nicole sympathized.

"I'm exhausted."

"City boy ain't used to this kind of hard work," Wes claimed.

"City boy has more sense than to drive his truck into a wash! I saw the whole juvenile display from the ridge! What do you estimate that stupid coyote cost you, five hundred?"

"Doesn't matter, once I saw the expression on that old dog's face I knew I had to get him."

"He's gone over the hill!" Richard confided in Nicole.

"Yup, he looked just like old Magelby," Wes continued.

Nicole giggled. There was a resemblance between the two.

"...and around the bend," Richard was still describing Wes.

Wes was smiling, his sour mood was gone. Richard was mad. Mad at Wes for turning a nice drive in the desert with Nicole into a nightmare filled with long hours of incessant labor in the hot sun without food or water. Mad at Nicole for laughing at Wes' stupid jokes about it all. Richard sprawled out and folding his arms across his chest closed his eyes and pretended to go to sleep. The sun was down and darkness began to descend quickly upon the desert. The steady hum of the pickup began to lull Nicole and she grew sleepy. Although her eyelids grew heavy she continued to watch the road mile after mile as though hypnotized.

"There's a coyote!" Wes' voiced boomed out in excitement.

"No, damned you!" Richard exploded. "We haven't got a spare!"

"I just remembered," Wes sighed in disappointment. "I'm outa shells."

Nicole had been watching the road and hadn't seen a coyote. Wes hadn't slowed the truck at all. A quick glance at his face confirmed her suspicions. Her face revealed to Richard the fact that he had been had. Late that night the truck pulled to a stop in front of Nicole's. Richard got out and walked Nicole to the door.

"Thanks for the day, Richard. It turned out to be quite an adventure."

"Adventure?" Richard was incredulous. "I wouldn't call slaving in the hot sun all day an adventure!"

"Well I enjoyed being with you anyway," Nicole gave him a peck on his dirty cheek and turned to go inside.

"Wait!" Richard caught her by the arm.

"Hey Dicky! You gonna stand there and kiss all night? I'm hungry, I wanna go home," Wes called from the truck.

"Oooooh," Richard grated, "that S 0.B. is the most exasperating person I've ever known. Wait for me."

Richard stalked out to the pickup. Nicole could hear the two men arguing. The engine was shut off and Richard returned to her. Taking her by the arm he guided her around to the back of the house, carefully putting the building between them and Wes. Richard guided her into the orchard and stopped her among the fruit trees. He positioned her so he could clearly see her face in the moon light. She could see his face soften as his thoughts turned away from his previous irritation. He bent and tenderly kissed her.

"Nicole, I had hoped to give you this under better circumstances but I am leaving to go back to school tomorrow and I won't have another chance."

Richard drew a small white package from his pocket and handed it to her. It had been beautifully wrapped but the bow was smashed and the paper smudged. His face was full of excitement.

She carefully unwrapped it and opened the small velvet covered box to reveal a large and beautiful diamond engagement ring. Even in the pale moonlight it sparkled with fire.

"Oh Richard it's beautiful!"

"Try it on."

Once it was or her finger Nicole held it up to the moon light and admired it.

"I love you, Nicole, and want you to be my wife!" His voice was soft but full of emotion.

Nicole put her arms around him and pulled him close and looked over his shoulder into the night.

"Does that mean yes?" Richard prompted.

"I'm so surprised. I hardly know what to think," Nicole evaded.

"Do you love me? You've never said so."

"I love how you look, you're so handsome and sexy. I love to be held and kissed by you. I love the way you move."

"It's settled then?"

"Give me a little time, Richard. The idea is still so new. I need to be sure. You'll need time to make your peace with Linda and Amy," Nicole was correct in assuming the mention of these two names would create the desired diversion.

"Linda's about given up," Richard hesitated.

"And Amy?"

"I'll tell her at the proper time. There is no need to hurt her unnecessarily."

"No, I guess not," Nicole took the ring off her finger and put it back in the box.

"Keep it until you decide," Richard urged. "While you are deciding take it out and look at it and think of me."

He took her in his arms again and kissed her passionately until she was breathless and weak kneed.

"I think we had better go back," Nicole's voice was low and husky. Richard was smiling confidently as he walked her to the house. The night was spent waking and tossing with emotions in turmoil as Nicole tried to sort out her feelings. Richard was very attractive to her, as she had told him, but she had not been able to say, 'I love you,' with no reservations. Was she afraid of her own emotions? His proposal had thrilled her but there was still that nagging doubt. Days later she was still confused but she had grown accustomed to the turmoil and was able to sleep.

Learning that Wes was going to go to Reno for three days she finagled an invitation to ride with him. An invitation to stay with Richard's family was quick coming forth once she talked to Richard on the phone. Conversation with Wes dwindled as the long miles slid slowly by. Wes was preoccupied with his thoughts and Nicole's were in Reno with Richard and the dilemma that awaited her there. Curious as to why Wes had the camper shell on his pickup with mattress, pillows, and blankets in abundance Nicole began to joke.

"Should I be worried that you are planning to run out of gas?" Nicole gestured towards the rear.

"What? Oh, I'm just waiting for the perfect spot," he joked back half-heartedly. He volunteered no information but withdrew back into himself.

Richard greeted her at the door with an eager but quick kiss and drew her into the house. Wes followed with the luggage. The elegant house sat on a large, well kept lot, the interior was richly, but tastefully done. The place was immaculate with not a piece of lint or a particle of dust to be seen. Nicole wondered how a house could be so spotless with people living in it.

"Mom, Dad, this is Nicole," Richard said with pride. Mom had short blond hair with dark roots, brown eyes with an expression that denoted humor, even mischievousness, and a pretty but practiced formal smile. Dad was older with graying hair and a friendly but tired smile. He looked at Nicole with appreciation. They had responded formally.

"Nicole, these are my parents, Stephanie and Gerald Straussmen, and this is my little sister Mildred."

"Millie," the slim, young, blond woman corrected.

She wasn't as fine of feature as her mother but the bloom of youth compensated amply.

"Hello Stephanie, Gerald," Wes had stepped up beside Nicole. The greeting was polite but there was a tension in the air.

"You've grown up, Millie," A strange timber crept into his voice as his hungry eyes drank in her image. Millie carefully presented a cheek to be kissed to satisfy protocol.

"I'll be by late Friday afternoon," Wes reminded Nicole as he turned to leave.

"Wes," Stephanie had stepped over and placed her hand on his arm, "will you stay for dinner?" She had spoken as if it was mere form but her touch on his arm was almost a caress.

Suddenly this strange scene made sense to Nicole. Stephanie was Wes' ex! As Wes declined and left in retreat, Richard had taken Nicole's luggage in one hand and her hand in the other and was saying,

"Let me show you to your room."

The room was large and airy with a canopied bed in the center with yards of white lace. A closet lined one wall, mirrors the opposite wall. The bathroom was ample. A large screen T.V. and V.C.R. sat on an oak table. The phone on the night stand completed the picture. Though not as large, the room reminded Nicole of the bridal suite in a fancy hotel. Richard pushed the door shut and put her luggage down, then took her in his arms and swung her around in a dance step. Spinning her under his arm he neatly guided her back on to the bed. Instantly he was down beside her with his lips on her neck and his hand caressing her back and shoulder. He cut off her protest with his mouth on hers. Moments later his mouth was on her neck and her struggles had ceased.

"Richard, we shouldn't," Her fingers were in his hair holding his head close. She moaned softly. Richard moved his head back and propped himself up on his arm and watched her. Moments later her eyes fluttered open.

"I love to turn you on," He smiled at her. "I only quit because I know you would feel rotten later and you would hate me. That's just the way you are."

Nicole got up and moved around the room to get away from him, to regain her composure.

"Why didn't you ever tell me that Wes is your father?"

"You didn't know? Everybody in the valley knew that, I assumed you did to."

"Everybody else must have assumed the same thing. Millie must be Wes' too."

"That's right. Who did you think I was?"

"Wes' brother, you quarrel like siblings," Nicole pointed out.

"I know. I can't help it. Wes is always playing these stupid tricks on me. Well he plays them or everybody. Nobody is safe. Wait till he starts on you."

"What kind of tricks?"

"For example, a lady called and said that there was going to be a free clinic to test for hearing loss. They were going to be in town on a certain date and time, and she asked if Wes would like to have his ears tested. Well good ol' Wes said,

'Pardon me?' Well, the lady raised her voice and repeated herself. 'Come again?' Wes said louder. Each time she spoke, Wes answered louder as if he couldn't hear. He had the poor gal thinking that she had a customer if only she could communicate. She was screaming at the top of her lungs, 'I think you need hearing aids!' Wes answered, 'Hearing what?' 'Aids,' she screamed back, 'You need aids!' 'Thanks just the same lady,' he answered in a normal voice, 'but what fool would want Aids, even if it's free?' And he hung up."

Chapter 7

Nicole had a great time for the three days with the Straussmens. There was a concert the first night, a floor show at a fancy casino the second night, and the third night Richard took her dining and dancing. Although they showed interest in her life in the valley and asked her many questions, there was always a lull in the conversation whenever she mentioned Wes' name. She learned quickly that to speak his name in this household was considered bad form. Nicole was still lounging in bed Friday morning when Stephanie entered, shut the door behind her and sat on the bed.

"When I lived in the valley, we had nothing to live in but an old trailer. What does the place look like now?"

"I don't know," Nicole answered. "I've never been there."

"Richard has told me but men miss so much when it comes to details about decor. Tell me, is there anyone in the valley for an older man to date?" Although Stephanie hadn't mentioned Wes' name, Nicole understood that she wanted to talk about him.

"Wes took my mother out once."

"Are they good friends?"

"I think so, but mother's romantic

preference lies elsewhere. Mother is a refined and cultured person and Wes, well you know Wes," Nicole spread her hands.

"Yes. My father moved to the valley to become the high school principal. He too was a man of refinement and culture. When I became interested in Wes, he wasn't pleased, but I was young and head strong. Wes and I married right out of high school. My family stayed only two years in the valley. My father moved from there to Reno and has been much happier where the life style is more in keeping with his sensitive nature. Wes bought that little trailer that I mentioned and moved us out into the most desolate spot in the valley. He drove truck in the winter and tried to farm and ranch in the summer between trips. He had more than he could do when he decided to build us a house.

I was alone most of the time for those two years. Richard and Millie were born by the time the foundations and preliminary plumbing was in the ground. Wes was killing himself trying to provide what he thought I wanted. When Wes was sent to jail I felt completely abandoned sitting way out there in the desert, miles from town with two small children to care for. Wes had purchased a few animals and I had to feed and care for them also. It was too much to ask a young wife to do. I sold the animals and moved here to Reno to be near my parents. During the months that Wes was in jail I was asked out a few times. It was then I met my present husband. He took care of the details and I was divorced and remarried by the time Wes was released."

"What did Wes do to get thrown in jail that time?" Nicole wondered.

"He was operating a short wave radio without a license. They confiscated his radio and fined him. He refused to pay and they threw him in jail. He insisted that the government had no right to curtail his right to freedom of speech. Of course I asked Gerald and he said they had the right to regulate business and communications for security reasons, Gerald would know, he is a lawyer."

Recognizing that Stephanie had come in with the need to talk about Wes, Nicole encouraged her.

"What was Wes like when he was younger?'

"Wes was a lot of fun to be around. Everyone liked him, his being center on the basketball team didn't detract from his popularity. Even then he was quite rebellious. He was looked up to as some kind of hero, but of course the rest of us grew up and became responsible citizens. Being married to him I soon learned that he had a narrow, small town mentality. I could clearly see that he would never change. Stephanie, when she had entered, had an almost wistful need to find out about Wes but as she reviewed their life together she had remembered the reasons she had left him and convinced herself once again that she had done the right thing. Nicole also thought that perhaps she had begun her campaign to have Nicole on her side if she were to become a member of the family.

"Richard said something that made me think he didn't know Wes until recently," Nicole commented.

"Richard decided at the end of school year that he would like to know Wes. He hadn't seen him much since he was a small child. From the little bit he has told me, Wes is as exasperating as ever. I don't understand why Richard keeps going back, unless it is to have a place to stay while he courts you," This last thought was comforting to Stephanie. She smiled at Nicole.

After lunch, Richard came in to visit her while she packed.

"Leave the door open please," She smiled at him.

He made himself comfortable on the bed. He grabbed her left hand and examined the naked ring finger.

"Have you decided yet?"

"I'll tell you what; when I decide, I will wear the ring for you to see."

"Do you have the ring with you?"

"Yes."

"Are you tempted?"

"Yes."

"Why don't you put it on? I didn't get a good look when we were in the dark."

"Are you trying to trick me?"

"Who, me?" Richard placed his hand on his own chest and looked so innocent. They laughed.

Later in the day Millie motioned her over and handed her the hallway phone. Voices could already be heard so she didn't speak. Millie walked away down the hall.

"Look, Angela honey. I told you how it was going to be this week," It was Richard.

"How much longer is she going to be there?"

"She's leaving early this evening."

"Are you coming over to see me tonight?"

"Can't I come over tomorrow?" Richard sounded reluctant. This pleased Nicole.

"You don't want to see me," The feminine voice was petulant.

"Of course I do, it s just that I have been up late three nights and I'm tired."

"I bet!"

"We went out as a family. I've told you how it is."

"Is she pretty?"

"In a wholesome sort of way."

"Do you see her when you go to…. Where ever it is you go?"

"I told you Wes is helping that widow get a handle on things with her ranch. We have to go over there some times. I can't help but see her."

"Was your social duty pleasant?" Angela's voice bordered on sarcasm.

"She's three years older than I, practically an old maid. Look, Angela, I'm give out and grumpy. Let me get a good night's sleep and I'll call you first thing in the morning."

Nicole smiled; Richard had slept until nearly noon and was a spry as could be.

"You don't want to see me," There were tears in the voice. Richard sighed.

"All right, you can come and see me tonight about eight. I'll take a nap. Wake me up when you get here."

It was becoming more apparent all the time that Richard had a hard time saying no to a woman. He wasn't used to a woman saying no to him either. Smiling, Nicole hung up. Wes came at five to pick her up. Richard checked her finger once more before she left. Stephanie was very cool toward Wes but Nicole noticed that she swallowed hard when he went out the door. Wes put Nicole's luggage in the back. Not a word was said for a long time as they drove through the city.

"Did you have a nice time?" Wes had become uncomfortable with the silence.

"Yes, I did. The Straussmens were very nice to me."

"I'm sure they were," Feeling that the social form had been filled, Wes fell silent again.

"Stephanie told me a little about your life together."

"Did she now?" Wes asked with a marked lack of interest.

"I think she still cares for you. It must have been hard to spend all those months alone."

"Her friend drove the kids to her parents in

our car. Stephanie rode with a truck driver she met. She didn't arrive for a month. I had been in jail for three weeks."

Nicole had succeeded in hearing the other side of the story.

"I guess a person never quite gets over experiences like that. I know Stephanie hasn't."

"It hasn't bothered me for some time now. I haven't even thought about it since a week ago Wednesday," Wes said facetiously.

As they reached the outskirts of the city Wes slowed and made a left. Several minutes later he stopped in front of a modern apartment house.

"I won't long."

"I need to go the ladies room," Nicole informed him.

He got out and walked around the car and opened the door for her but he didn't seemed too pleased. They walked to the door and Wes rang the bell. A look of anticipation crept onto his face. Nicole standing to one side couldn't see who answered the door.

"Oh, hello Wes. You're early," The sweet, feminine voice protested mildly. "May I present my fiancé Travis Spencer?"

The look of anticipation had been replaced by one of hurt and anger. This expression in turn, with an obvious effort, was overcome by a closed polite one. Wes took Nicole's hand in his big rough one and pulled her into the light from inside.

"This is a close friend of mine, Nicole

Defoe. Nicole, this is Sophi Wesly," Wes introduced her. "I guess you heard his name," Wes gestured at the other man. It was Sophi's turn to struggle with her facial expressions but she managed beautifully. The painful introductions were over and Wes and Nicole were invited to enter and to be seated on the sofa.

"May I use your bathroom?" Nicole asked. Sophi nodded her assent and ushered her down the hall. Once they were alone, Sophi made no effort to hide the hostility in her eyes but she was still very proper and polite. With her dark, proud, little head held erect and hands folded in front of her slight built body, Sophi stopped in front of the bathroom door. Eyes, made to appear almost black by the flash of white, surveyed her carefully as if Nicole was the enemy, but the full-lipped, sensuous mouth was smiling sweetly. As Nicole closed the door behind her she could hear Sophi calling,

"Girls come and see who's here!"

Squeals of delight followed the sound of small feet pattering down the hall to the front room. Minutes later, Nicole rejoined the others to find two dark haired, dark skinned charmers seated on Wes' lap, chattering excitedly. A third little girl clung shyly to her mother's leg but was watching Wes with only one eye peeking around. Wes playfully dumped the two onto the couch and slid to the floor on all fours. He approached Sophi slowly with a low growl in his throat. The two girls from the couch leaped onto his back for a ride. Completely hidden now, the other girl cowered in delicious anticipation. Still on hands and knees, Wes moved around Sophi and reached out with long claw like fingers to grab his tiny prey. She shrieked and ran around her mother. Wes stopped and went the other way. This maneuver was greeted by another shriek. After several attempts, the game was still at stalemate. Wes then thrust his arm between Sophi's legs, narrowly missing his quarry. Sophi's dress rode up as she was bumped off balance. Sophi laughed, but quickly squelched her laughter when she remembered Travis. She captured her daughter and swung her onto Wes' back behind the other two girls. Wes gently circled around and pretended to try and get the girls off his back. They were having a great time.

"Come now girls, it's time to get ready to go," Sophi finally interrupted, "I know your dad has a long way to travel yet tonight."

She pulled them off from Wes' back and began herding them down the hall.

"Can I be of help?" Nicole offered.

"Yes, of course, if you wish," Sophi accepted stiffly.

It quickly became evident that Sophi felt it necessary to send her daughters with Wes looking their best. Their dresses were carefully selected to match not only their own outfit but to coordinate with that of their sister's. Bows were carefully attached to long straight gleaming dark hair. Shoes were carefully polished. Sophi, with a wet wash cloth, cleaned away smudges that were almost imaginary. Quick, efficient little hands of a dedicated mother darting here and there, made Nicole feel clumsy and inexperienced. All the while Sophi visited politely but without the slightest hint of warmth or interest.

"Do you live the valley?"

"Yes, I've lived there for about a year and a half."

"Where did you live before that?"

"Boston."

"How do you like living in the desert?"

"I've come to love it."

"Have you known Wes for very long?" This question was asked without change of inflection but the tension in the room was more pronounced. It occurred to Nicole that Sophi was jealous. Also, it became clear at that point that the reason Sophi had arranged to have Travis there was to prove something to Wes. Nicole's presence was completely unexpected.

"About a year," Nicole answered.

"It takes a long time to really know Wes," Sophi made this sound like some sort of warning. The three little girls were lined up in front of the mirror while Sophi fussed over the final details.

"Now you mind your daddy...and Miss Defoe," Sophi instructed her daughters. "I assume you will be helping Wes," she addressed Nicole.

Full, undisguised hostility was now in Sophi's eyes. By this time Nicole was feeling very uncomfortable. Not only was she helping in a deception, but she was receiving Sophi's unearned malice.

"I believe there is some misunderstanding between us," she stated.

"Oh?" Sophi wasn't giving an inch

"I am Richard's girl friend," Nicole clarified.

"Richard?"

"Wes' son."

"Oh yes, Richard. He must be all grown up now."

"Yes, and very handsome."

Suddenly Sophi laughed. She was embarrassed.

"You must think I'm awful. I'm sorry," she apologized.

"It can't be an easy situation for you. I think I understand in part," Nicole assured her.

"That is just like Wes to misrepresent you like that," Sophi accused.

"It was purely an instinctive defense maneuver. He didn't even invite me in, but I told him I had to use ladies room," Nicole felt the need to defend Wes.

Sophi not knowing how to respond to this without appearing argumentative quickly changed the subject.

"I'm not being very polite. I didn't even introduce my children. The oldest is Veronica. She is six. The next is Amber, she is four, and the baby is Gina."

"How old are you?" Nicole bent down to the little girl.

In response, she held up three fingers.

"She is not," contradicted Veronica, "she's only two."

Gina's little eyes carefully inspected her tiny hand then carefully she folded down one finger and proudly held up the remaining two.

"That's right!" her mother complimented.

"Time to go, don't run," Sophi smiled at Nicole with an open friendly expression as the girls slowed to a hurried walk. What a contrast in the two men who had made small talk while the women were getting the kids ready. Travis was small, compact and cocky while Wes was large, loose jointed and ill at ease. Travis was handsome and fine of feature, Wes had coarse rugged features. Obviously the smaller, younger man was well dressed and sophisticated while Wes considered himself dressed up in new work clothes.

At the sight of the girls dressed and ready to go, Wes was relieved. Travis was amused at Wes' relief.

"Here are some diapers for Gina," Sophi began explaining to Wes. "She is potty trained but is still a little shaky at night."

Nicole and Wes walked the girls out to the truck. Wes returned for the luggage.

"I get to sit by the window," Hollered Veronica.

"I get to sit by daddy," Yelled Amber.

Little Gina was beginning to look panicky at the thoughts of leaving her mother and going with people she didn't know that well. Nicole took her onto her lap and tried to comfort her. Gina curled up and popped her thumb in her mouth. Sophi had followed Wes out onto the stairs.

"Have a nice trip and don't spoil the children," she admonished, "and Wes, it would be easier on everybody if you wouldn't play these little charades," Sophi had to let Wes know that he had been exposed.

"And it would be a hell of a lot easier on everyone if you weren't so damned pulchritudinous!" he boomed back in anger. Sophi's little chin came up and her hands folded in front of her in her peculiar stance of defiance. Wes stomped down the stairs and Sophi turned back inside and firmly shut the door. Wes drove like he was trying to prove a geometric axiom; the shortest distance between two points is a straight line. Several times other driver's had to brake or swerve in self defense. Wes' jaw was set, his eyes fixed on some point in the distance. Nicole didn't feel entirely safe.

"Daddy, I lost my new shoe," Amber's big sad eyes looked an appeal at Wes.

"Nicole , would you see if you can find her shoe," Wes asked impatiently.

After a thorough search Nicole admitted defeat.

"There is a mall up here. We'll stop and buy her some new ones," Wes decided. He wasn't about to go back to Sophi's. Once in the mall Wes gave instructions.

"You take Veronica and Gina and go that way. I'll take Amber and go this way. If I find a shoe store I'll stop and buy em. If you find one, keep on walking around until you meet me. Then we'll come back to it."

Nicole walked around until she found Wes sitting with Amber as the salesman tried on the new shoes. Nicole sat outside near a fountain and waited. Soon Wes came toward her with Amber dancing and skipping proudly in her new shoes. Wes looked unhappier than ever.

"Where's Gina?" he demanded. Nicole was shocked to discover that Gina was nowhere in sight.

"She was right here a second ago!" Nicole was suddenly in a panic, "kidnapped!" was the first thought that came to mind.

"I'm sorry Wes! I'll find her!" Nicole promised.

"You go back around that way. I'll go back around, this way." Wes strode off with Amber in tow. Nicole grabbed Veronica by the hand and walked rapidly in the other direction. As she made the loop, a large group of people, gathered in front of a display window were pointing and laughing. Inside the store was another group.

"Oh, no!" Nicole laughed as she spotted Gina.

At that moment Wes strode up.

"Did you see her?" he demanded.

Nicole pointed into the store. Wes plunged through the crowd into the store as Nicole watched from outside. Just as Wes reached the display of bathroom furniture, Gina caught sight of him and slid off her perch.

"I went pee-pee in the potty, Daddy!" She shuffled over to him with her panties still around her ankles. A puddle was slowly growing on the floor beneath and around the fixture. The crowd was hilarious. Wes knelt gently down and pulled up Gina's panties and straightened her dress. At that moment, a young man in a colored smock approached.

"Do you work here?" Wes asked.

"I'm the manager."

"If you have a rag or something I'll mop up," Wes offered calmly even though his neck and ears were bright red.

"I'll do it," The manager grinned. "The show was worth it!"

Wes snatched up his daughter and fled, the crowd parting to let him pass with only a few good natured gibes. Back on the road again, Wes drove mile after mile with his eyes fixed on the road in the distance. The girls got bored, then sleepy. Wes pulled to the side of the road, got out, opened the door of the camper shell and transferred the girls onto the mattress.

"Would you rather stay back here and get

the girls to sleep or would you rather drive?" he asked Nicole.

"I'll ride back here for a while."

Nicole told stories until they were asleep. The motion of the truck soon put her to sleep also. Some time later she awoke and opened the little windows between the cab and the camper.

"Would you like me to drive for a while?" she offered.

"I'm alright," Wes declined.

"I'll ride up front and keep you company,"

Wes stopped and waited for her to get in the front then resumed the journey. He still stared down the road with that fixed stare. They rode for a long way in silence. Nicole recognized where they were as they dropped off the high desert mesa into the long narrow oasis of the valley.

"What does pulchritudinous mean?" she asked.

Wes' dour expression suddenly changed to one of sheepish mirth and a chuckle escaped him. But he said nothing.

"Come on Wes, let me in on it."

"Look it up," he responded. "I'm not sure if I remember correctly."

Several weeks had passed since the night Wes had driven her back from Reno. He no longer came to advise Roark and her mother and he had ceased to come to the bank. Nicole guessed that his trip to Reno had been a trying experience. She learned from Richard that the little girls had gone back home after a brief stay. Richard called on a regular basis but he never wrote a letter.

"Hello Nicole, I miss you," Richard's voice was low and intimate.

"I miss you too."

"Enough to spend a weekend with me?"

"Where?" Nicole asked cautiously.

"Wes'. Sophi is getting married the week after school is out. Wes has agreed to take the kids while she goes on her honeymoon. She is going to drive the kids down and I am going to ride down with her. We will be coming by your place about nine in the evening. You could come down to Wes' with us and spend the weekend."

"Does Wes know this?"

"Sure. He had a, devil of a time with the kids last time. I think he would appreciate your help. Besides, I think he would rather not be alone when Sophi comes."

"What makes you say that?"

"I don't know for sure, just a feeling."

"Richard, there is something I've wondered about for sometime. Isn't your family well to do?"

"I guess you could say that."

"Didn't you tell me that little metallic green sports car was yours?"

"That's right."

"Then why are you always hitching a ride with someone else when you come to the valley?"

"Last summer when I wanted to come and spent some time with Wes, he agreed on the conditions that I leave everything at home and come and work for him at a cow hand's wages. He said he didn't have time to tend some teenage playboy. I think he said that thinking I wouldn't come."

"Does that still apply?"

"I guess. He has never said anything to the contrary."

"For all your complaining about how Wes treats you, I think you enjoy staying with him."

"I have to stay some place when I want to see you."

"There are motels here which I'm sure you can afford and if you didn't stay with Wes you could drive that little car you're so proud of. Besides, you'd be much closer."

"Ah, now I know where this is leading. You want me to be close at hand in case you find you can't stand to live without me for another minute."

"I think it's safer for you to stay with Wes. I take it that Travis isn't coming?"

"Travis?"

"Sophi's fiancé."

"No, he is attending a bachelor party that weekend."

Chapter 8

Finally the day came when Richard was out of school and Nicole waited impatiently for the hour that he had said they would stop by for her. She still wasn't sure it was a good idea to spend the weekend with him, but on the other hand, she hadn't been able to resist. Her mother had seen the little velvet case and had guessed that it contained Richard's diamond. She had let it be known that it would be alright with her if Nicole chose to marry him. An occasional comment designed to elicit information had been ignored by Nicole.

Shortly after sundown, headlights shone in the front windows, followed promptly by a knock on the door. Nicole let it be answered by her mother.

"Come in Richard. It's good to see you back in the valley," Mrs. Defoe was smiling in a most friendly manner.

"It is good to be back. You don't know how lonely I've been," Richard and Nicole's mother exchanged a knowing look.

Nicole thought of Angela and rolled her eyes before she entered the room, but put on a bright smile for him. Richard carried her overnight case out to the car and stowed it away in the trunk.

He stole a kiss before he opened the door to the car. Sophi was radiant despite the long drive. She too greeted Nicole cheerfully. The children were already dressed in their pajamas and were comfortably settled in the back seat with blankets and pillows. The long monotonous miles coupled with the quiet rhythm of the big new car had lulled them to sleep.

For the next forty-five minutes, Sophi chatted amiably while Nicole snuggled under Richard's arm. Despite Richard's best efforts to conceal them, Nicole noticed that he was casting admiring glances in Sophi's direction. For the first time, Nicole saw the park surrounded by the trailers owned by Singletree. There seemed to be plenty of visitors tonight. A short distance past these, Sophi turned off the highway onto a gravel road. Another fifteen minutes and a large squat looking, two story house loomed into the head lights.

The large arched portico and stucco walls reminded Nicole of the adobe haciendas she had seen in pictures of old Mexico. Walls, strong and solid looking that ran to the back, both on the north and south, gave the impression of a small fortress.

Sophi organized the transfer of goods and children into the house; Richard carried Amber, Nicole Gina, while Sophi awakened Veronica enough for her to stumble in on her own with the aid of her mother's guiding hand.

"Oh, Mommy," Veronica exclaimed in her sleepy little voice, "We're home!"

Wes greeted them at the door and directed Richard and Nicole with their human cargo. Sophi guided Veronica to her room. Nicole laid the sleeping baby in her bed and carefully tucked the covers up around her chin while Wes waited inside the door. She straightened up and moved out into the hall. Glancing back she saw Wes gently duplicating her motions. Back in the living room, a strained atmosphere put a definite damper on any conversation. Wes asked Sophi to show Nicole to the guest bedroom, and indicated that Richard follow him. They exited to the left rear of the house while Sophi turned out the lights and led Nicole to the right, down the hall where the children were sleeping.

"We have been sent to bed," Sophi smiled sardonically.

"This is the master bedroom. I will be sleeping here. If you need anything just let me know. And this is the guest room. It has its own bathroom. The men will be sleeping in the worker's wing, as Wes calls it; as far from the women as possible. He can be very old fashioned," Sophi sounded almost sarcastic.

There was nothing left to do but go to bed.

"Exciting weekend," Nicole muttered.

Breakfast was served early. Wes made it a boisterous, fun affair centered on the girls. He teased and tickled until they had nearly forgotten to eat, but finally they were full and ran out to play in the court yard behind the house under the shade of the sprawling branches of the huge trees within the walls.

"Richard, you are to feed," Wes instructed the moment they were gone. He arose and immediately left also.

"Wes!" Richard protested in vain.

Nicole was left alone with Sophi as Richard stomped out to do his assigned task. Not wasting a motion Sophi moved quickly about the kitchen, cleaning, washing and putting things away. She knew where everything was and where everything belonged. She directed Nicole, keeping her busy also, mistress of the house in manner if not in fact. It occurred to Nicole that Wes and Sophi must have separated only a short time before she had met Wes at the casino.

"There, the kitchen is clean. Next come the bedrooms," Sophi declared.

Leaving a mark in the light coat of dust on the top of the chest of drawers she announced,

"The place is filthy." For the next couple of hours Nicole ran herself ragged trying to keep up with the energetic little woman as they moved from room to room.

"It's time to be thinking about lunch," Sophi glanced at her watch.

"I'd like to see the rest of the house," Not only was this true but Nicole also thought it would be a nice rest to stroll through the rooms. The tour wasn't restful. Sophi marched through the house explaining what little needed to be explained and telling Nicole a precise, chronological order of when each room was finished. Nicole, as she observed the thick walls, heavy timbers and Spartan furnishings, thought how much like Wes was the architecture; strong, simple, yet appealing.

"If I had been here longer I would have decorated this pile of mud until it was livable," Sophi declared.

Coming in from feeding the animals, Richard passed Nicole as she went out to get the girls. She had received the assignment of getting them washed up for lunch. It was a bigger chore than she had supposed. Finally they were presented at the table to be inspected by their mother. Surprised at the rapidity with which Sophi had placed a large and appetizing meal on the table, Nicole was about to compliment her, but there was Richard, his admiring eyes following Sophi as she moved about the kitchen. Taking his admiration as her due, Sophi was smiling and visiting amiably. Richard laughed at the slightest witticism. Neither seemed to notice when Nicole entered. Surprised at herself, Nicole acknowledged that she was jealous.

It was apparent that lunch was ready but Sophi delayed seating everyone, her eyes discreetly checking the window for Wes.

"Mommy, I'm hungry," whined Amber.

"Let's eat," Sophi directed. "Wes knows it's lunchtime I'm sure. He'll show up if he's hungry."

"When ol' Wes gets to cutting hay he wants to cut just one more windrow before he quits. Then it's one more round, then just this patch. He might be hours."

Richard's exposure of Wes' personality was greeted with a knowing laugh from Sophi. Thus the fact that Wes was avoiding Sophi and that she was waiting, wanting something from him, was lightly glossed over. As the afternoon passed Sophi postponed the planned departure time. Richard continued to try to avoid being obvious in his desire to be in her presence but Nicole thought he was making a fool of himself.

"Don't you have to feed the animals in the evening to?" she finally reminded.

"Yeah, I do," He looked at his watch. "I have just enough time before dark. It takes about three hours."

With this explanation, he quickly left. Sophi smiled in amusement at Nicole's maneuver.

"Wes is right," Nicole responded in irritation,

"It would be a lot easier on everyone if you weren't so damned pulchritudinous!"

Sophi's little head came up in defiance. Her hands folded in front of her and her back became ramrod straight in her peculiar fighting stance. Suddenly Nicole laughed.

"Come here," she commanded.

Sophi, looking puzzled, followed her to the library.

"What are you looking for?"

"Dictionary."

Sophi pointed. Nicole pulled down the large volume and thumbed through it.

"Here it is. Pulchritude: comeliness, beauty. Pulchritudinous: having or being marked by pulchritude."

A strange, but pleased look began to creep over Sophi's face. Nicole couldn't help but laugh.

"I didn't know what it meant either. I thought that Wes was insulting you too."

Darkness had fallen over the valley. The children had been fed and were in their night clothes when Wes finally came in from the fields. He showered and dressed and came to dinner but said very little and finished quickly. The rest of the evening he spent playing with his daughters He gave them horsey rides and played hide and seek until Sophi declared it was their bedtime. Wes stretched the rule long enough to read them a story then packed each one to bed and tucked them in.

Immediately upon returning to the front room he excused himself and retired. After a few minutes of polite conversation Sophi excused herself and went to her room. Still piqued at Richard for paying her such scant attention all day, Nicole followed suit. She undressed and sat near the window in the dark to catch the cool evening breeze. Of the four adults in the house, Nicole was sure that at least three of them were sitting in their respective rooms, wide awake as she was. Wes had worked steadily all day and perhaps was tired enough to sleep but Richard hadn't worked that hard and he was a night hawk, and Sophi? She obviously was after some thing and would be busy planning how to get it. There was something eerie about four people sitting silent in the dark house each with his own thoughts. At that moment Nicole somehow knew that Wes wasn't asleep either.

A soft rapping at her door startled her. She moved silently and leaned close to it.

"Who is it?" she whispered.

"Who else could it be?" Richard's voice whispered back.

"Richard," she whispered back fiercely, "after today you don't have any right to make innuendos!"

"After today?"

"Don't give me the innocent act, Richard. I think it's positively indecent for a man to look at his stepmother that way."

"You mean Sophi?" Richard sounded incredulous. "She's ten years older than I, practically an old maid."

"Tell me the truth Richard," Nicole sounded dangerous. "Do you, or do you not, find Sophi to be beautiful?"

"Yes, I do, for a woman her age I think she is quite well preserved but sweetheart you are the one that I'm in love with, O.K.?"

Richard s voice had taken on a gentle sincere quality that had its effect.

"May I come in, Honey?" he asked humbly.

Nicole put her hand on the doorknob, only

to feel it turn ever so slightly. She realized that the only reason he was not already in the room was because the door was locked.

"No."

"You don't believe me," she heard him sigh sadly.

"I'm not dressed," she informed him.

"Do you remember how it was at the pond last summer?" he persisted. "Remember how good it was to feel skin against skin?" Nicole swallowed hard at the memory but didn't answer.

"Remember how it was at home in Reno in your bedroom on the bed? You didn't mind then. Don't you trust me? I stopped of my own accord, remember?"

"I trust you every bit as much as I trust myself."

"Then what's the problem?"

"That's the whole problem! Good night Richard." She could feel his presence on the other side of the door for several long moments before she heard his soft tread moving down the hallway. She walked carefully in the dark, back to her chair on trembling legs and sat down. She wiped her sweaty palms on her panties and leaned back feeling weak. Even while she had recognized that he was sweet talking her, she had nearly succumbed. Luckily he had been barred from placing his lips on her neck and his hand on her bare skin or she knew she would have been helpless. Slowly the mood passed and her strength returned. Moving to the window she sat on the wide ledge to catch more of the breeze. Her heart jumped within her as a shadow suddenly moved in the moonlit courtyard. There was no mistaking Sophi's slim, proud, graceful figure as it glided silently down the stone path and came to a stop before another shadow. What had been a dark blob in the night began to move and the silhouette of a large loose jointed man sitting on a bench was easily seen.

"Do you still find me pulchritudinous?" The quiet female voice drifted on the night breeze.

"Body and mind," came the equally quiet but gruff reply.

"You're pulchritudinous too!" Sophi sat a straddle of Wes' knees, and taking his face between her hands kissed him with a long intimate kiss.

"Take me into the house!" Sophi sighed.

"I no longer have the right."

"Yes you do! No one has ever possessed me but you, darling," Sophi vowed feelingly.

"I know Sophi. You've always been a good girl that way."

"What's a little piece of paper between you and me?"

"There is an old law that demands order in all things. Without it, there is confusion over who owns what and to ignore it breeds malice and hate, even blood shed."

"You're not afraid surely?" Sophi taunted gently.

"No, but if you were mine all other men

should fear me."

"I've never understood this thing you have for the law."

"No Sophi, you never have."

"Let's get married, Wes, tonight. We could drive into town and wake up the Justice of the Peace!" The excitement was high in her voice.

Wes didn't answer.

"Don't you love me? I know you do!" Sophi's voice betrayed her panic.

"Yes, sweetheart, I love you."

Unlike the generic word spoken to Nicole, 'sweetheart' spoken to Sophi was full of love, desire, regret, and pain.

"I love you too, Wes. You know I do."

"Yes, I know."

"Then there is nothing to stop us."

"We've tried it three times already. It wouldn't be any different this time."

"It was my fault. I'll be different this time. Remember how happy we were when we first moved here? And that first time we got remarried and moved to the coast? Even this last time it was wonderful until after Gina was born. We could move away to where no one knew us and have a new start."

"I remember. I remember how easily you made friends. Both men and women instinctively like you. You say the right things, you are interested in people, and you are generous with your time. You're fun and interesting and beautiful. People confide in you knowing that you will be discreet. I've always been so proud of you, proud to be seen with you. I always thought that your life was like a colorful flower garden with me sitting like a sagebrush in the very middle of it."

"What are you saying?" Sophi asked in dread.

"The trunk of sagebrush is all twisted by adversity, its leaves dull and colorless. You are ashamed of me Sophi, ashamed of who..."

"No!" Sophi cried covering his mouth with hers to stop the words she couldn't bear to hear and truths she had never been able to face. With great passion she covered his face with kisses intending to burn away his thoughts with her love and desire. She pulled his face into her neck. Wes nuzzled her and moved his lips downward to the hollow of her shoulder. Nicole watched as the robe fell from Sophi's body revealing bare shoulders and legs.

With face turned to heaven, eyes closed and mouth slack with passion, Sophi now knelt on the bench pressing Wes against her. His head moved in slow rhythm with the soft moans and sighs.

"Wes!" Sophi gasped, "Don't make hickies on me!" All motion ceased immediately.

"Don't stop! Wes, please!" Sophi pleaded.

Sophi was set gently but firmly on her feet as if she were a small child. Wes bent and retrieved her robe and draped it around her shoulders, all without speaking a word. Sophi turned and walked away with measured pace, her bearing erect and proud, but as she passed near Nicole's window, the moonlight fell on a contorted, tear stained face. As Nicole turned away to her bed, her own face was stained with tears and a painful lump filled her throat.

"You poor, foolish, blind woman!" she cried out softly. As a result of her eavesdropping on the painful love scene in the court yard, Nicole began to realize that relationships between man and woman were nothing to be entered into lightly or blindly. It was obvious that Sophi found Wes immensely attractive physically, but she had chosen a man that would be socially acceptable.

Richard was immensely attractive to Nicole physically, but what of all the other aspects that make up a marriage? They had never been discussed. How did a couple know before hand if they would be happy together?

She began to closely scrutinize the budding romance between Roark and her mother. Roark had been elevated to the privilege of having dinner with them as a means of discussing the problems associated with running the ranch, but more and more, other subjects began to take up the time. It occurred to Nicole that Wes had dropped completely out of the picture. He never even stopped by to say hello. The more she thought of the mismatch between him and her mother, the more the suspicion grew that Wes had used his pretended interest in her mother as a means to advise Roark who was an inexperienced manager and to build him up in the eyes of her mother who had feared that Roark had been looking after his own welfare at the expense of the ranch.

At the risk of putting himself in a position to be ridiculed, he had succeeded in saving the ranch from financial ruin. This coupled with the fact that he was so much in love with Sophi convinced Nicole that her reasoning was sound.

"Mother, were you and daddy happy together?" Nicole asked one night after Roark had left for the night.

"Yes we were."

"Was the difference in age a big hurdle?"

"Perhaps the greater experience of your father added to our compatibility."

"Do you think you would be happy if you married Roark? If so, why, and if not, why not?"

"Nicole, I'm tempted to say it is none of your business but I perceive that you are thinking of you and Richard."

"I so confused. Why are some couples so in love after forty and fifty years, while others can't seem to find anyone they can live with?"

"Divorce is caused by selfishness on the part of one or sometimes both. Lack of self-control is perhaps the greatest symptom of this common malady. Little cutting remarks disguised as humor is another manifestation of this basic problem."

"Is Roark selfish?"

"In a few little things but it isn't a serious character flaw. I guess I'm selfish too, in some ways."

"How important is physical attraction?"

"Speaking for myself, I could never marry a man that didn't ignite a romantic spark in me no matter how good or kind he was," Nicole's mother confessed.

"Me either," Nicole agreed." Does Roark qualify?"

"Yes, but that doesn't necessarily mean there will be a wedding."

"How about Wes?"

"He is attractive in a rough, wild sort of way, but he has a horrible reputation. I'm afraid he would be fatal to any woman's happiness."

"And Richard?"

"Of course you will have to decide for yourself but I find him to be a very attractive package."

Not a long time later, Nicole found herself seated in Wes' pickup with the very attractive package himself. They were parked on the mesa with the lights of the valley twinkling on the valley floor below them. Richard reached for her.

"Richard, I need to talk for a minute," she evaded him by sliding over next to the far door. Richard shrugged.

"Richard, I want you to know that you are about the most attractive, sexy man I have ever met. I've never been so ah...ah...affected by ah..."

"Turned on," Richard supplied the phrase.

"Yes, thank you. I have always had fun with

you and you have always been very sensitive to my feelings. I have no regrets whatever and will always look back at this time in my life and treasure it. However I feel it would be unfair, even dishonest to keep this any longer," Nicole extended her hand toward him with the velvet box in the flat palm.

He turned his head away and blindly gazed out into the night. Carefully she placed the ring on the seat between them and waited.

"I thought things were going so well between us," His tone of voice indicated that somehow she had deceived him.

"I've always felt very flattered to be number one on your list," Nicole gently reminded him that the relationship had never been exclusive on his part. "You'll always be number one on my list," he vowed.

"But there will always be a list," Nicole thought.

"Have you ever considered moving to the valley permanently?" Nicole changed the subject.

"Not really. It's a hard place to make a living. I've got prospects in Reno that would be the envy of any man."

"The valley is an excellent place to raise children don't you think?"

"Yeah, I guess, but it's awfully expensive to raise kids now days, even in the best of circumstances."

"You do want children don't you?"

"Sure, a kid or two would be alright but any

more would only be a burden in today's economy. Do these questions have anything to do with whether you will marry me or not?"

"No, I've already made up my mind. If only you had been raised in the valley here with Wes," Nicole said with sincere regret.

"I don't understand these vague references you're making. If you've got something to say, say it plain."

"My greatest desire at this moment is to part friends."

"Part friends?"

"Although I find you so physically attractive I can hardly keep my hands off you, I'm not going to marry you. It's best to say goodbye."

At a loss for words to describe his frustration and hurt, Richard started the vehicle and headed towards Nicole's.

"I guess Sophi went through with her marriage?" Nicole broke the long silence.

"Yes. There was big article in the society page. She did alright by herself."

"I'm sure she did."

Another long silence descended upon the couple, lasting until they pulled up before Nicole's door.

"Don't get out, Richard," Nicole let herself out and walked around to Richard's open window. A short, hard, emotion packed kiss was her only goodbye. She turned and fled into the house. The little velvet box lay on the seat where Nicole had left it, unclaimed and ignored during the long, lonely drive home.

Chapter Nine

Advertisements were plastered on the fences, walls and telephone poles throughout the valley. There was to be a celebration. Dinner! Games! Entertainment! Fireworks! Dance! It was the Fourth of July and the whole valley was in a festive mood, but for Wes it was just another work day. He had come home to his big empty house, rifled through his nearly bare cupboards for something to eat, and taken a long hot shower. Now he stood dressed in an old pair of warm-up pants from his high school days, in front of a steamy mirror, scraping the water softened whiskers from his face, when a rare knock came on the door.

"Come in!" his big voice boomed through the house.

"Hello, Wes."

Wes turned to the voice from the bathroom doorway.

"Richard ain't here. Amy come by earlier and took him to the festivities."

Nicole only nodded.

"Let me tell you something about the Wesly men," Wes continued as he contorted his face and stretched his skin tight to make it easier to shave off the stubble.

"There ain't a one of 'em that understands women, see? Now you take that little Amy. She knows you have to whack a Wesly male in the middle of the forehead to get across the idea that she likes him, see? In my opinion you are the more attractive of the two and I'm sure Richard thinks so to, but, you are inclined to be more laid back and to let things take their course. Uh-uh." Wes wagged his razor at her to indicate this wasn't the proper procedure.

"From my observation the women think Richard is something but I think he is insecure. He needs quite a bit of encouragement. Now, my advice to you is... be a little more forward and let him know he has a chance with you and I'd bet anything you'd have him right where you wanted him, see?"

Nicole smiled as Wes turned again from his shaving and emphasized his point by making a chopping motion toward her with his razor. He turned back to his shaving and immediately cut himself. Nicole was making him nervous. Washing the soap and blood from his face, Wes turned toward her but instead of moving to let him out the door as he expected, Nicole stepped forward, wrapped her arms around his waist and buried her face in the black curly hair of his chest. After what seemed like a great while of standing surrounded by a great stillness, Wes finally responded by slowly bringing his arms up and placing his hands gently on her shoulders. Only then did she dare raise her eyes to his face. The look of startled amazement, so strong in his expression caused her to giggle.

"I'm in love with you, Wes," she said. "It

sneaked up on me too."

"You poor woman," Wes sighed sadly, his hands patting her in a comforting, consoling manner.

Nicole realized that Wes blamed flaws in his own character as the cause of his two previous failed marriages and that she would have to work until he felt at peace with himself before a permanent relationship between them would be possible. In light of recent events in his life, this loomed as a formidable task.

"I'm gonna get dressed," Wes removed her arms from around him and urged her toward the door with his hands.

"Would you take me to the fireworks?" Nicole had resisted in the doorway. Wes, it suddenly became clear to her, was embarrassed to be half clad in her presence.

"Yeah, I guess," Wes acquiesced in part, simply to get her out of his bedroom. Thirty minutes later Wes opened the door of his pickup to let Nicole in. There on the floor was a litter of wrenches, hammers and other tools necessary for mechanical repairs. On the seat lay a pair of dirty gloves and a greasy pile of rags. Wes glanced at Nicole's white slacks and hesitated.

"We could take my truck," Nicole offered.

Again Wes hesitated, but finally spoke.

"I have a better solution," He walked around to the side of and some distance from the house to a shed. Nicole followed out of curiosity. A large door slid to the side to reveal a gleaming red VW bug. Wes opened the door and with a large clean rag kept inside, he wiped the seat clean.

"You'll have to drive this thing. My feet are too big to operate them tiny pedals."

The little car fired right up and Nicole backed out to give Wes the room to swing the door open and climb in. Humming down the road Nicole noted how much fun the little car was to drive. It had been kept in immaculate condition despite the fact that it was many years old. Only a light coat of dust indicated recent neglect.

"There's a coyote!" Nicole exclaimed as she let up on the gas and began to drift to a stop.

"My rifle is in the truck," Wes informed her without the slightest trace of excitement. The reason for his despondency suddenly came to her mind.

"Was this Sophi's car?"

"Yeah."

The very fact that they were riding in it indicated to Nicole that although Wes had kept it in perfect shape for Sophi in hopes that someday, somehow things would work out; he now recognized the reality and finality of their last encounter. Why hadn't she taken it with her when she left? Nicole guessed she would feel more comfortable in something more prestigious. They rode in silence, Wes not in the mood to talk and Nicole felt that he required none from her. She was comfortable with it.

For a small town the fireworks were fairly

spectacular with the loud explosions and the profusion of many mixed and varied colors streaming through the sky. Only a few inconsequential remarks passed between them the whole time. Slowly she became aware that Wes was being very careful in everything he said. In place of his normal exuberant offhand way of approaching things, he now weighed everything before it was spoken. Gone was the humorous bantering and arguing that had been so much a part of the many trips she had taken with him and Richard into the desert to check the grass and water holes for the cattle. It came as quite a shock to realize that he was now scared to death of her, even as he treated her with kid gloves in order to avoid hurting her feelings. Had it been a colossal blunder to declare her love in such an open and abrupt manner?

Once the fireworks were over, Nicole drove past the large open sided pavilion in the middle of the city park where the dance was being held. Already the live band was in full swing as the dancers moved vigorously around the floor. The picnic tables had been moved out onto the lawn under the trees where the old folks sat and watched and gossiped. Children ran playing games just outside the circle of light.

"I'm thirsty Wes. Can we stop and see if there is any punch?"

Near the one end of the pavilion next to the massive stone fireplace there was a refreshment table. As Wes and Nicole skirted a small mud puddle and stepped up onto the cement floor they passed a line of men standing with their backs to the rock work.

"Well, look who is sniffing around Singletree's bashful little whore," said a voice from the line followed by a few chuckles.

"Saves him the time and expense of slipping over to his neighbors," another voice replied.

Guffaws followed this remark. Much to his surprise the man on the end of the line found himself staring up into Wes' angry face. Wes had crowded up close, leaving no where to escape.

"What was that?" Wes growled.

"It weren't me!" was the stammered response. Wes immediately moved to the next in line.

"Was that you?"

"No."

Each man in turn denied having spoken until Wes stood in front of the last man. Having been released from Wes' threatening bulk, each of the others had melted away into the uncertain light.

"Well Rhino, it must have been you. I want to hear an apology for the lady," Wes' voice was deadly.

Rhino's face became sullen and stubborn. He refused to answer. Without warning Wes' arm flew into motion. Frieker in an effort to ward off the blow threw up his arms and jerked his head back banging it hard on the rock wall behind him. However Wes' motion ended with him smoothing down his hair. Stepping to the side to allow Frieker to stagger forward a step Wes then crowded him to the edge of the floor. Wes' left swung around low and Frieker leaned away and jerked his hands down to protect his belly throwing him off balance. His foot stepping off the foot drop from the floor was enough to send him over backwards to flop heavily in the mud.

With his left hand Wes stood scratching his own belly. He had never touched his victim. Rhino crawled out of the mud and sloshed angrily away under the hard stare of his adversary.

"He strikes me as a high strung, nervous feller," Wes remarked to Nicole with a wicked gleam in his eye.

It was abundantly clear to Nicole that the snide remarks of Rhino's friends were calculated to incite Wes into a brawl wherein they could collectively give him a severe beating, but he had diffused the attempt by focusing his attention on one at a time. Singly, each one lacked the courage to try Wes. The slander on her reputation had not gone unchallenged nor had Wes given any cause for Rhino to take him to court again.

"Well done!" Nicole complimented.

Wes seated her at a table and brought her a drink. They sat and sipped as they watched the dancers and the other activities about them.

"Care to dance?" Nicole took the initiative after a twenty minute interval.

"You have a mighty short memory," Wes

answered.

"No, I don't," Nicole raised her foot for him to see.

A dainty cowboy boot with heel and toe capped in metal with a mirror finish was held up for his examination.

"This is beginning to look like a well planned operation," Wes said without changing expression, but he rose, took her in his arms and swung out into the crowd on the dance floor. It was fun whirling around and being held in his arms.

"You love dancing, don't you?" she said into his ear.

"I might if I didn't do it so poorly."

"Nonsense, you just lack confidence."

It was a wonderful night for Nicole with music and lights, darkness and fresh air but mostly being close to Wes and feeling his warmth and smelling his aftershave. She began to be aware that other people were noticing them. Her mother had a quizzical look on her face as Wes swung her gently in a half circle. Even as Richard swung Amy's pert little figure under his arm, his eyes followed Nicole with a strange cynical look on his face.

"Sorry," Wes had stepped on her toe. She hardly noticed.

"Didn't feel a thing, relax and enjoy." Nicole began to rub her hand softly up and down his back.

"That ain't relaxin'," he declared after a moment, his voice gruff. She looked up into his face but his expression belied the tone of his voice, the shadow of a smile softened his features. Despite himself, Wes liked having her in his arms. Immediately after the number was through, Nicole felt a hand on her elbow. She turned to find Richard claiming a dance. He swung her away with the start of the music, leaving Wes alone in the crowd.

"Where is Amy?" Nicole asked.

"She stepped out for a breath of fresh air." Nicole laughed.

Richard had chosen a dance that would allow him to hold Nicole close. He didn't speak for a while but finally his desire burst out.

"I've missed you," his voice showing more emotion than he had intended.

"I've missed you too," Nicole answered honestly, but her emotions were different than his.

"Maybe we could try it again."

"I'm afraid not."

Richard didn't speak again until he had kept her for another dance.

"You come with Wes?"

"I did."

"I can understand why he would ask you but.... well I guess you didn't want to sit home alone," Richard's fishing expedition was successful.

"I drove down to Wes' and invited him," Nicole clarified.

Having watched Nicole dance with Wes he could see that it was more than a desire to avoid a lonely evening but he had to hear it from her own mouth before he could believe it.

"So the old man has beguiled another young beauty," Richard had intended this to be sardonic humor but it was accompanied with a bitter cynical laugh. He left her abruptly. Nicole danced a few more times with Wes before he suggested that they go. Claiming thirst she managed to linger a few more minutes but soon they were on their way. No sooner had they reached the outskirts of town than a red light flashed and a siren blared in their ears. Nicole pulled over and waited. A young officer got out of a deputy sheriff's car and approached.

"May I see your driver's license?" he asked politely.

"Not yet," Wes instructed her. He got out and walked around the car and stood facing the officer.

"Why are you stopping us?"

"License plates expired."

"Don't you know that is against the law of the land to stop a freeborn citizen in his right to travel? I can see that you don't. We'd like to see your identification," Wes informed him

"My identification?" the officer said in dismay.

"I've lived here all my life and I've never seen you before. I think you are an impostor."

"I've only been on the force for two weeks," the officer explained.

"Likely story. Keep that rifle on him Nicole. If he moves, blow his guts out. Keep your eyes on me!" Wes barked as the officer's eyes began to shift to Nicole.

"That's better. Now raise your hands." Once he had complied, Wes unfastened the strap and removed his pistol. Pointing the pistol at him, Wes directed,

"Carefully and slowly take out your wallet and give me your I.D."

With pale face and shaking hands the officer complied. Wes took the I.D. and handed it to Nicole.

"What's your name?" Wes demanded.

"Harold Mercer," He nervously licked his lips.

"Weight."

"One hundred seventy-five pounds."

"Height."

"Five foot eleven.

"Is that right Nicole?"

"Yes."

"Drivers license number."

"I,ah I don't know,"the officerstammered."

"He doesn't know his driver's license number," Wes said significantly.

"Badge number."

"Eight, four, seven, ah, four....eight, four seven..."

"He doesn't know that either," Wes looked menacingly at the young man. "I'm afraid things are going to go pretty hard on you son."

Wes opened the back door to the officer's

car and waved him in. Once he was locked securely in place behind the screen Wes climbed in front and spoke into the radio.

"Captain Wareing... Captain Wareing , please."

"Captain Wareing here, go ahead."

"Captain, this is Wes. I was pulled over by some criminal posing as a deputy sheriff. I've got him locked up here in the back."

Nicole could clearly hear Wes' side of the conversation.

"How do I know he's an impostor? Well, first off, he doesn't know that a free born citizen has a God given right to travel. Second, he doesn't know his badge number or his driver's license number."

Wes stopped to listen then responded.

"Well, he has a furtive look about his eyes and a very nervous manner, a real criminal if I ever saw one and he kinda slouches, not at all like an officer of the law." Again Wes stopped to listen. Nicole then heard him read the description from the officer's driver's license. Wes got out and released the officer and handed him the mouth piece.

"Officer Mercer," he reported. "Captain, the guy doesn't have his car licensed? I pulled him over and asked to see his driver's license and his wife points a rifle at me and he disarms me and locks me up. He's some kinda loony if ya ask me."

"Wait a minute," Wes protested. "let me talk to the Captain. Captain," Wes began once he had jerked the mouth piece from the deputy, "this guy is lying through his teeth! I don't have a firearm of any kind!"

The argument raged for several more minutes with Nicole hearing only two thirds of it. Wes returned to the car and sat quietly.

"What's happening?" Nicole asked'

"Officer Mercer insisted that the captain come out to settle the argument over the rifle. He wanted him to see for himself," Wes explained.

A short time later another car pulled up.

"May we search your car?" Captain asked Wes politely.

"Certainly," Wes agreed.

A quick but thorough search turned up nothing.

"But I swear she had one," Officer Mercer protested.

"Did you watch carefully while I was driving out here?"

"Yes."

"Could they have slipped it out of the car?"

"No, they just sat there."

"Could they have disassembled it and hid the pieces?"

"No."

"Then where is it?"

"I don't know but…"

"Did you actually see the rifle or did someone perhaps suggest to your mind that there might be one?"

Officer Mercer did not answer, as for the first time the awful truth began to impress itself upon him.

"When you were hired you were given strict instructions to leave this man alone," the Captain bawled out the officer.

Officer Mercer had a stunned look on his face.

"Yes," the captain informed him, "this is Lionel Wesly."

"I didn't know and he was breaking the law. We should arrest him."

"Pursue it if you want, but in this case it will be you that will end up in jail and when you get out you won't have a job."

The unhappy officer got in his car and left, his superior turned to Wes.

"I trust there will be no more heard about this incident from your side if there is nothing from ours."

"No harm done. Everyone must learn from his own experiences," Wes replied philosophically.

"What was all that about?" Nicole asked as they drove away.

"I didn't want you to get a ticket for driving my car with out a license," Wes grinned at her expression.

The atmosphere was much more relaxed on the return trip and Wes seemed more like his old self, laughing and gently teasing. Nicole drove the little car into the shed, got out and waited for Wes to close the shed door. He didn't invite her in although the hour was still early, but stood a bit awkwardly as if waiting for her to take her leave.

"I believe that was the most interesting date I've ever been on," Nicole commented.

"That's nice, sweetheart," he answered.

"Don't call me that!" Nicole regretted it the instant it was out of her mouth but she couldn't stand the flat emotionless word in contrast to the love filled expression used for Sophi. All easiness evaporated between them and once again Wes was carefully choosing his words.

"I'd better go," Nicole moved toward her pickup.

Wes held her door for her while searching for an appropriate goodbye.

"Thank you for the date, Nicole." He was so formal that Nicole was surprised that he didn't punctuate his sentence with a bow.

"That is about as bad," Nicole assessed.

"I knew a barber named Nick. That wasn't his real name, just his nick name," Wes offered.

"That would be fine," Nicole laughed.

Late that night Nicole lay in her bed thinking of the night's events. She thought of the confusion she must have caused in Wes, first saying she loved him then denying him the courtesy of calling her Sweetheart. Later, her mind turned to the episode with the policeman. Who was Wes that new recruits were warned to leave him alone? She drifted off to sleep before her mother got home.

Late the next morning Nicole sat down to breakfast with her mother who had slept much later than normal and still looked like she hadn't had enough.

"My word mother, what time did you get in last night or should I say this morning?"

"You have your roles mixed up," her mother evaded. "That is the question mothers ask their daughters."

"I got in before my carriage turned into a pumpkin but I bet yours was baked into pies and consumed before you got in," Nicole speculated.

Her mother didn't confess but changed the subject.

"You danced with Wes quite a bit," her mother observed. "Did you leave with him?"

"Yes, we went together."

"Nicole, it doesn't take a genius to see that you and Richard have had trouble but to seek revenge by dating his father is a childish, if not to say, a dangerous stunt. I'm not going to allow you to mess up your life like that."

"It was all over between Richard and me before I even considered Wes. It wasn't out of revenge."

"Even so, for a man of that age and experience, and believe me, he has experience, you should hear some of the things I've heard about Wes, to pursue an innocent young girl is absolutely deplorable."

"He isn't pursuing me. I went over and

156

asked him to take me to the fireworks."

"What's gotten into you, chasing after men like that? Why, in my day, that was unheard of!"

"Girls ask guys out all the time now."

"Maybe boys they have grown up with, but not men twice their age whom they scarcely know, who have been in and out of prison a half dozen times and who have been married about that many times and who are the biggest trouble makers in the county and who have children scattered all over the state who..."

"Who went to prison to save me from a savage mauling by a brute and who went to prison to defend the right to work and to help old neighbors who can't help themselves!"

"You'd defend this man?"

"Any man that would hold himself up for ridicule to save a widow's ranch deserves a friend."

"What do you mean? You aren't suggesting that Wes saved me from ruin? Roark is the one that has done the work here. He has told me that Wes came pretending to help just to get in good with me. He can't help but be in financial trouble with all his attorney's fees and all the time he spends in jail. He had his eye on my ranch. That's the truth about Wes! He's nothing but a gold digger! Are you suggesting that Roark is lying to me?"

"No but..."

"You can't have it both ways."

Nicole sat quiet, knowing that the argument was lost, nothing she could say would change her mother's mind about Wes.

"If you are determined to be friendly with Wes I can't stop you, but I won't be a party to it. He is not welcome here nor are you to use my vehicles to chase down there after him. After all you are still my dependent and I am still responsible for you."

Nicole wanted to point out that her mother had depended on her for that miserable time while she had worked at the casino and later on when she first went to work for the bank but recognized that this had been a difficult thing for her mother also and would only cause hurt and another argument.

"I understand," she said.

"That's better. With the passing of time you will get over your upset with Richard and will be able to think more clearly. Someday you will thank me for this, believe me."

Eight days later, Mrs. Defoe parked the car next to the curb in front of the bank and waited for Nicole to get the small case from the back. Once on the curb next to her mother's window, Nicole leaned in the window and hugged and kissed her.

"I love you," Nicole had tears in her eyes. "I won't need a ride home tonight. I've found a place of my own."

Stunned, her mother for a long time in silence.

"How will you get around?" she finally asked.

"I'm close enough to walk to work, the grocery store and the movie house. I can afford and

I am looking for a used car."

"And your things?"

"I have what I need," Nicole indicated the small case she had been taking to work everyday for the last eight days. "I'll come for the rest of it when I get a car if I am permitted."

"Of course you are," her mother cried. "Why Nicole, why this way?"

"I'm assuming full responsibility for myself in order to be free to make my own decisions."

"I can understand that, but why the deception?"

"To make certain that the break was clean and simple with no misunderstandings. I recognize my debt of gratitude to you for bringing me into the world and raising me all these years. If the time should ever come that you need care I hope to be permitted to provide it."

"How can you cut me out of your life like this?"

"You may visit any time you like. Here is my address." Nicole handed her a card already prepared for this very purpose. "Gotta run. I'm late."

Nicole hurried away up the walk, leaving her mother sitting slumped disconsolate. That evening with a sense of adventure, Nicole approached the tiny house that she had rented. Once inside she walked through the rooms that she would now call home noting with satisfaction that everything was organized according to her needs.

The front room was large enough to seat two guests, the kitchen table would seat two people, and the bed room would sleep two in the double bed. A bathroom which contained the utilities completed her domain. Nicole estimated that it would require no more than thirty minutes a day to keep everything clean and orderly. Although the furnishings were drab, the little house appeared to be in good repair, giving her the feeling that she had made a good bargain, for her rent was minimal.

Preparing dinner and cleaning up the dishes only took a few minutes of her time, leaving the evening free. Silence settled in on her with a comfortable friendliness as she put away the last items from her case. She curled up on the couch with a book. By the time she tired of reading, the friendly feeling of silence had lost its appeal to be replaced with a feeling of aloneness. The long evening stretched unrelieved before her.

This was not the first time she had lived away from her mother but always before there had been plenty of roommates coming and going to assure that she would never lack for considerable social activity in her life. For the first time she felt isolated. Had she been a fool to leave her comfortable, easy life at the ranch for the remote possibility that Wes would court her? He had made no effort to contact her in the three weeks since the Forth of July. She stifled the impulse to call her mother. The thoughts of Wes sitting in his home all alone was almost more than her will power could handle, her eyes incessantly returning to rest on the phone. But she didn't call for fear Richard might answer. She had no T.V. On the list of things to buy she wrote 'Radio.' After puttering aimlessly about for a few minutes Nicole gave up and went to bed, only to toss and turn restlessly. Finally she drifted off to sleep.

Chapter Ten

Mr. Trimble was waiting for her with an air of suppressed excitement as she arrived next morning for work.

"I've found you a car!" he exclaimed. "It s in excellent shape but he no longer wants it and is willing to sell it for a lot less than it's worth! It gets good gas mileage and has relatively few miles on it."

"What kind is it?"

"VW."

"A red one," Nicole stated.

"Yes." Mr. Trimble was a little disappointed that Nicole already knew about it.

"It belongs to Wes I assume?"

"Yes it does."

"Did Wes tell you he wanted to sell it before you told him I was looking for a car?"

"Yes. He came by last night and said he wanted to sell it. He said he had no use for it."

Nicole had no trouble guessing why he was selling it but of he was willing to sell it to her did that mean that he felt certain it wouldn't come back to him? She felt certain that Mr. Trimble would have explained that she needed a car because she now lived in town but Wes hadn't come to see her. It was unreasonable to expect him to but still her feelings weren't changed by reason. Seeing that her employer had made a special effort to help her,

Nicole covered her reluctance with a smile.

"Thank you. It is a fun little car to drive. Wes let me drive it once. I'll call him and tell him I'll buy it."

Mr. Trimble was pleased. Arrangements were made and later in the week Wes was sitting in her small front room trying to sustain polite conversation while he waited for his ride to pick him up and return him to his ranch.

"It's a good little car," He was talking like a used car salesman although she had already given him a check.

"It is sound both body wise and mechanically, very economical."

"It will be fine, Wes. Thank you. I know it is worth more than I paid for it."

Wes looked away embarrassed. He twirled his hat in his hands. Richard's metallic green sports car pulled up outside to furnish relief from the tortured conversation.

"I see Richard is traveling first class these days," Nicole observed.

"Yeah, he is mad at me. I guess I imposed too strict conditions on his staying with me. He has moved into town."

A horn blared its impatient message.

"He's mad at me too," Nicole confessed. "Is he still working for you?"

"No."

"What is he doing?"

"Bumming, I guess," Wes sighed. "Its tough

having your kids call another man daddy all their lives but its even worse having them adopt ideas foreign to your own."

"What do you mean?" Nicole probed.

"Years ago knowledge was sought to maintain a moral and free people but now everything is based upon economic considerations. Feathering your own nest has become more important than anything else. I was hoping Richard would raise his sights but I guess after twenty one years of indoctrination it was too much to expect."

Once again the horn blared impatiently. Wes rose.

"You better have the ant-freeze checked when you stop by to fuel up next time," He advised her on the care of her new bug.

For a long time after he left Nicole sat and contemplated the ironies of life. Wes, her mother, Richard and herself were all sitting in their individual house alone, each isolated by his own desires. Her mother had forced her out by trying to run her life. Nicole sat alone to be free to pursue her relationship with Wes. Wes sat alone because he feared that she had marriage on her mind. Richard sat lone in retaliation against Wes' apparent conquest of Nicole. If only she had been able to accept Richard, All this wouldn't have happened.

Her guilt and self pity were narrowly averted by the thought that Richard wouldn't be alone. A more thorough examination of the situation lead her to believe her mother would be even more interested in marrying Roark now that she didn't have Nicole's company nor responsibility for her. As for her feeling for Wes she would just have to be patient. She sighed. At best it would take a long time to overcome his reluctance to become involved with another woman.

Mid-morning of the following day Nicole overheard Mara, the other teller, visiting with a customer.

"That's too bad about what happened to Carlos last night."

"I haven't heard," Mara answered.

"He got beat up. Wes has already been in town to see the sheriff."

"Who beat him up?"

"Nobody knows. Wes' other workers were scared off by persons unknown, but Carlos refused to run. He's in no shape to work now. Wes can't get anyone to help drive his cows out of the hills and the forest service has threatened to load them up and haul them out and bill Wes for the expense. Of course Wes says he won't pay and is taking the Forest Service to court."

"On what grounds?"

"Apparently the Forest Service claims that the range where Wes has cattle grazing permits is too dry and needs a chance to recover. Wes, on the other hand, says that the Forest Service is singling him out for persecution because none of the other ranchers have to pull their cattle off the range."

Ten minutes later Nicole had reached her

decision and was standing in Mr. Trimble's office in front of his desk.

"Yes, Nicole, what can I do for you?" he asked pleasantly.

"I would like some time off."

"I'm sure that can be arranged, when?"

"Immediately."

"You mean right now? How long would you be gone?" Mr. Trimble scowled.

"I don't know." Nicole then explained the situation Wes was in.

"Have you any experience in working cattle?"

"No, but I'm a good rider." It was true she had become a good rider.

"I doubt you would be of much help," Mr. Trimble responded.

Though Nicole was insulted at his assessment she merely said,

"Wes has done a lot for me, I need to help."

"Go ahead then, but if you want time off every time Wes gets into trouble you'll be a mighty busy person," Trimble grumped.

"You don't fool me," Nicole told him. "You act so cynical but you help out too when it's needed."

"What do you mean?"

"Who paid the fine for the old man that got fined for having Wes fix his roof?"

"Who told you that, Wes? Wes himself

166

helped pay that fine."

"Wes and who else?" Nicole pointed her finger at Turnbill.

"Well don't go blabbing it about. I have a reputation to protect."

Next Nicole went down to the motel. There was no where else for Richard to be staying. She asked at the office which room he was in.

"There is already someone there," she was informed.

Nicole walked down and knocked on the door. After a time the door opened wide enough to allow Richard to stick his face out.

"Oh, hello Nicole," His eyes were alive.

Nicole wondered what she had interrupted. She quickly explained the situation.

"I'm going to go help," she finished.

"That's nice of you," He was waiting for her to leave.

"I thought you might like to know," she said awkwardly.

"Yes, thank you."

"Richard! He needs help!"

"I'm not free right now," Richard defended.

Nicole turned away, angry at him for his lack of concern and angry at making a fool of herself. She stopped at the house to change into Levi's and boots then hurried down the road in her bug. Minutes later she noticed in her rear view mirror a car rapidly overtaking her. With long blond hair flying in the wind, Amy waved at her as she and Richard went streaking by. Nicole, when she arrived at Wes', learned that he had been ready to leave for the mountains as Richard and Amy had arrived. Already the goose neck stock trailer contained three horses and Wes was leading another horse from the corral. Richard was carrying another saddle from the tack shed. Amy was busy bringing more provisions from the house. A short time later with Nicole and Amy squashed tightly between the two big men in the cab of the truck, they were driving west on the high mesa towards the distant mountains.

Nicole had to move her knees back and forth to avoid the gear shift as Wes shifted while Amy sat snuggled under Richard's arm. Soon they were sweltering in the heat of a hot Nevada summer. After what seemed like an eternity, they finally climbed into the coolness of the pine forest. Wes geared down to climb up to the top of the first ridge on a dirt road that featured dozens of switch backs.

As the terrain leveled out they drove through beautiful, grassy meadows, surrounded by the stately pines and watered by small springs and seeps. As they approached the second ridge, a cloud of dust on the switchbacks ahead indicated another vehicle descending. Wes pulled his truck off the road into a small grove of trees and jumped out.

"Saddle the horses," he ordered as he found a spot to observe the distant vehicle.

"Forest Service," he identified it.

Immediately he went to his tool box and

selected a hammer and some short nails. He found a small, odd shaped board through which he pounded several nails. He positioned this in the dirt track and covered it carefully with dust then returned to the trees. The forest service truck shortly reached the meadow and sped up as the terrain leveled out. It too was towing a large stock trailer, but it was heavily loaded with cattle.

"Them are mine," Wes said without surprise.

The vehicle swept past, stirring up a cloud of dust as it began a long sweeping curve around the edge of the clearing.

"Damn," Wes swore, "It didn't work."

Just as the truck and trailer were about to disappear into the trees they came to an abrupt stop.

"Let's get over there," Wes swung up onto his horse. The others followed suit. It didn't take long to cut across the meadow to the Forest Service outfit, but by the time they arrived the Forest Service employees already had the punctured tire off and were examining it.

"Good afternoon, Jules," There was a deadly edge to Wes' voice as he addressed the solid square faced government official.

"Wes, how you doing?" There was nervousness beneath his jovial, confident manner.

"Them's my cows."

"Now, Wes. You know full well what the situation is. I'm only doing my duty."

"Richard, turn my cows out!"

"Wes!" Richard protested.

Nicole dismounted and turned toward the rear of the trailer. Jules moved to stop her but froze as he recognized the sound of a shell being levered into the breech of a rifle. Startled, Jules turned back to find himself staring down a bore that appeared as huge as a cannon from his perspective.

"Your lawlessness has gone too far this time, Wes. I promise you that your sentence will not be a mere few months this time! You're dealing with an officer of the Federal Government!"

Jules' confidence had returned, but the cows with their calves had already been turned loose and were spreading out on the meadow to graze.

"Jules, I can't believe that you would put yourself into such an awful spot," Wes shook his head sadly to emphasize his sympathetic expression.

"You must truly believe what you are doing is right. You must really not know that the Forest Service is an illegal organization run by a bunch of thugs bent on the destruction of the American tradition of freedom."

"What the hell are our talking about?" Jules raged.

"The Constitution states that the federal government shall only own enough land for forts, magazines, arsenals, dock yards and other needful buildings. You'll notice that forests are conspicuously missing from this list. When Nevada became a state, the deed to these lands legally should have passed to the state. Further more, I purchased, in good faith, enough grass for a specific number of cattle as determined by your own illegitimate employer. Now by change of policy, you seek to deprive me of my property. On top of that, you arbitrarily and without advising me, selected a date on which you would begin to confiscate my cattle to hold them for ransom. I, as a sovereign citizen of Nevada, arrest you for stealing my grass and rustling my cattle!"

"You've lost your mind!" Jules asserted.

"You have the right to remain silent, anything you say may be…"

"Go to hell, you crazy bastard!" Jules screamed. Ignoring the rifle still pointed directly at him, Jules turned and yelled at his two subordinates,

"Get in!"

"But Jules.....," one began to protest.

"Get in!" Jules jumped into the truck behind the wheel, started it, jammed it into gear and drove off the Jack with a bang. Wes turned away and signaled for his crew to follow. They rode away leaving the two hapless Forest Service employees to face the colorful high volume abuse being heaped upon their heads.

"Is it true, what you told the ranger?" Nicole asked once they were a good distance away.

"Definitely."

"Then why are we in such a hurry to get the cattle off federal lands?"

"If the government takes possession of the

cattle until this case is resolved, it is highly probable that I would never see them again. Statistics show that once property gets into their hands, it is rarely returned, even if they are sued and lose the case. In the meantime, I would be deprived of my livelihood and would have nothing with which to fight them."

"But how can they do that if they are operating outside the law?"

"Once the common people no longer understand the law sufficiently to demand that the government adhere to it, the government may simply choose to ignore it. The few that do know and revere the law are left to face the awesome power of the government virtually alone."

"You've got the law, they've got the power."

"Exactly!"

"I don't see how you have the finances to fight them anyway."

"There are six lawyers in this state who can see where we are headed and who noticed that I am willing to fight, but that I'm too dumb to ever win. They donate their time to my cases."

"Even at that, it seems to be like jousting at windmills."

"Sniper fire to make the soldiers on the firing line fearful of misapplying the law is about all we can hope for at this point. Jules doesn't give a damn if we sue the Forest Service. He knows we don't have the funds or the expectation of winning but if we sue him personally he has to stand the cost of his own defense. He'll find out that his employer isn't too eager to stand behind him. It's more likely that he'll be disciplined for misjudging the situation."

"Now I see why the local law enforcement is reluctant too mess with you."

Before they left the clearing Wes stopped and watched as the Forest Service truck started down the road at a pace unwise for the conditions. It was soon lost in a big cloud of dust. The horses were once more loaded into the trailer. Slowly they wound their way up the switchbacks to the top of the next ridge where it once more flattened out into lush meadows. Wes stopped the truck next to a large corral and loading chute that were full of cattle. Another Forest Service truck and trailer were parked near by.

"Hello gentlemen," Wes called to the four men that were in the process of loading another bunch of cattle.

"Wes," one acknowledged nervously.

"That was mighty nice of you to gather up my cattle for me but I've decided to drive 'em rather than haul 'em." Wes' manner was friendly.

"Wait a minute Wes. Our orders are to ship these cattle to the stock yards in town."

"Jules at this very moment is fleeing to avoid being arrested for cattle rustling. I'll assume that you were merely following orders with no intent to break the law but now you know the situation, you will have to be held accountable for what you do next."

"We better call Jules," One of the men walked to the pickup and spoke into the radio.

"Jules? Come in, Jules. He doesn't answer. Sometimes when you get down in one of these canyons the reception isn't too good. We'll try again in a while."

"We can't wait. Richard, let the cattle out."

This time Richard started to comply, but one of the men stepped in front of him. His companion who had talked on the radio shook his head.

"We better wait and see what's up."

The man stepped aside and Richard let the cattle out.

"Nick, you drive the truck down to where we left the other herd of cattle."

"I've never driven in the mountains. I'm afraid I'd wreck your truck," Nicole protested.

"Richard, you do it then. Push the cattle to the other side of the clearing. It will take us a couple of hours to join up with you."

They mounted up on the three horses that Wes unloaded and began driving the cattle across the clearing.

"Don't let 'em spread out too much," Wes shouted at Nicole. Nicole found herself racing back and forth desperately trying to control the cattle. Amy, on the other side of the herd with an occasional quick burst of speed kept the cattle moving with little effort. She was relaxed and yet when her horse wheeled or leaped into a run she seemed to be a part of it.

"Nick Spare our horse. He ain't a gonna last at that pace," Wes called.

Contrary to what Nicole had pictured in her mind, driving cattle was a lot more than a pleasant ride in the mountains. The cattle seemed to flow like water down the mountain following the path of least resistance but suddenly a steer would veer off toward a particularly lush bunch of grass, drawing several others with him. Any fork in the trail had to be carefully guarded to prevent the herd from splitting and arriving at different destination.

"Nick, watch behind you. Nick, keep 'em moving. Nick, there's no need to run the fat off 'em. They are getting away, Nick. Spare your horse, Nick."

It soon became obvious that Wes and Amy were doing the majority of the work, while Nicole was doing little good and at the same time she was killing herself and her horse. With great relief Nicole sighted the clearing where the truck was parked. Her relief was short lived as they paused briefly to let the cattle drink and to refresh themselves also. Richard had the small herd of cattle bunched near the trail that led away from the road. Richard was assigned to work with Nicole on her side of the herd. The two of them together managed do the work that Amy was doing by herself on the other side. Wes brought up the rear. It was evident that Richard had worked cattle before but he wasn't as proficient as Wes and Amy.

Nicole realized her condition wasn't as good as she thought. Already her rear and legs were getting sore from chaffing on the saddle. She was dusty, tired and feeling rather useless. It would feel great to soak in a tub full of hot water.

"Nick! Cut' em off!"

Nicole started out of her daydream to see a cow and its large calf trotting toward a trail leading off into a steep draw. She kicked her mount into a run to head them off but slowed up as she reached the point where the ground dropped off sharply. Of course the pair had broken into a run when they had seen her coming. They disappeared into the draw with tails held high in the air. Wes went by her and disappeared into the draw right behind them. Forty five minutes later he had succeeded in driving the animals over the ridge to unite them with the rest of the herd. His horse was lathered up with sweat.

Although he didn't say anything, it was obvious that he was irritated with her. She resolved that it wouldn't happen again. She edged up near the front of herd to keep the cattle from taking the wrong path. The leaders veered to the right toward a wide path that led over into the next draw that led toward the southeast rather than the north easterly direction they had been following. Instantly Nicole and horse were in motion, weaving back and forth and forcing the cattle down the northern draw.

It was several minutes before she noticed

Wes waving his hands frantically and Amy racing back and forth in front of the herd trying to turn them back. She suddenly remembered that Wes had pointed this trail out as the route that they had planned to go. Feeling extremely stupid she raced to help Amy. Finally the herd had been turned down the right path but not before the horses were blowing hard. The ridges on each side of the draw were steep and high, making it easy to keep the cattle in line.

"Nicole, ride back up to the truck and load your horse. Be careful, he likes to jump into the trailer, don't let him tromp you. Drive down the road to where you can see the foot hills end, then across to where you see this draw widen and flatten out." Wes was pointing out the route with his finger. "Drive up toward where we are now, there on the right side of the draw. You'll find a stream. Follow this up a short distance and you'll find a spring. We'll make camp there for the night."

The road wasn't as steep lower down on the mountain where the truck was now parked but it still worried Nicole, but she didn't dare say anything.

"Take your time. The distances are greater than they look from up here. You should beat us by a long ways."

Nicole did just fine until she was driving across the foot hills where everything looked different looking up the mountain than looking down. Forced to make a decision, she finally choose the draw that looked a little wider than the others and began to drive up a small track on the right side as she had been instructed. Soon the track was hardly discernible. She worried that she had turned up the wrong draw as she stopped and scanned the horizon towards the mountain. It was with great relief that she saw dust indicating that the herd was coming down the draw.

The track now had all but disappeared, forcing her to drive in low gear and weave slowly between the Juniper trees. By the time she saw the stream, the sun was down. When she arrived at the spring it was nearly dark. Gurgling from beneath a rocky protrusion the stream ran close to the ridge nearest Nicole leaving most of the flat on the other side. The stream bed itself was bordered by sharp rocky banks.

As she got out and stretched she watched the cattle emerge from the narrow draw onto the grassy meadow opposite her on the other side of the creek. It was with quite a shock she realized that they were walking down a small but well traveled gravel road. At that moment it occurred to her that as Wes had told her to drive up right side of the draw and pointing to his right he had indicated the south side of the draw. From the foothills looking up the mountain her right was the north side of the draw. She had made another stupid mistake. It was too late to go back down and drive up on the right side and there was no place to turn around! If she had driven up the right side she would have arrived in plenty of time to set up camp and start supper.

The cattle hurried past her to the stream and began to suck up water greedily, shortly followed by the three horsemen. Nicole watched Wes' dusty tired face as he took in situation. He sighed with discouragement but showed no surprise at what she had done.

"Amy, would you unsaddle the horses?" Wes asked politely. "Richard we'll need some fire wood."

Wes crossed the stream to where Nicole was standing.

"I'll cook supper; you lay out the bed rolls right over there." He pointed to a grassy spot on the south side of the stream.

Darkness descended before all the provisions could be carried over the stream. Nicole was quick to comply with the simple little requests that Wes made of her while he was preparing supper. She felt a keen embarrassment over her blunders that didn't diminish as the evening passed. She wanted to explain and justify herself but knew it would only sound like she was making excuses. She wished she had stayed home, she was of little use. Once supper was over Wes pulled off his boots and extended his feet to the fire.

"You better get dry or you'll get cold in the night," he advised.

After a time of sitting quietly by the fire, Wes outlined the sleeping arrangements.

"The men will sleep on the outside, the

women on the inside," Wes indicated the four bed rolls laid out on the ground cloth. He promptly climbed into his sleeping bag. Amy and Richard bedded down next to each other.

"I think I'll sleep over there," Nicole indicated a small grove of trees only twenty yards away.

"Suit yourself," Wes answered. "What shall I tell your mother if a mountain lion packs you off during the night?"

Richard and Nicole both looked nervously out into the inky black. Nicole thought she saw Amy turn away to hide a smile but she wasn't sure. She quickly crawled in between Amy and Wes. It wasn't long before she drifted off to sleep.

In the mountains near the desert, the hot air from the valley ascends up the canyons, creating a warm breeze in the evening, but later in the night after the hot air has risen, the cool air from the mountains rushes down the same canyon, causing the temperature to drop, cooling the desert with a canyon breeze.

Not quite awake in the wee hours of the night, Nicole could feel the chill creeping deeper and deeper into her bones but it took the movement beside her to awaken her enough to see and realize that Richard was taking Amy into his sleeping bag with him. Nicole, listening intently, decided that it was only for warmth. Nicole curled into a ball trying to conserve her body heat but found that she was shivering. She hadn't dried her feet thoroughly and now they were freezing her. She didn't want to admit to Wes that she hadn't taken his advice but finally she could stand it no longer. She scooted over next to Wes but found that his back was turned and that the insulation of the sleeping bags served to keep his body heat out. She was still freezing.

"Wes?" she whispered. His heavy breathing continued.

"Wes!" she whispered louder.

"Mmmm?"

"I'm cold."

"There are extra blankets in the trailer." His heavy breathing continued almost immediately.

Furious, she moved away from him but a few minutes later in desperation she got up, built up the fire, removed her socks and rolled up her pant legs. She waded the creek ignoring the sharp rocks and got the blankets from the trailer. Thank goodness the moon was bright. On the return trip she stepped on a thorn. She limped to the fire and sat down and dried her feet as she searched for the thorn. Her feet were dry by the time she found and removed it. She remade her bed and once again climbed in. She must have shivered forever but the next thing she knew she was being awakened and being told to climb out of her nice warm bed.

Breakfast was treated like any other chore, you got it over with as soon as possible and moved on to something else. Wes looked over the situation with the truck and decided he would have to come back later and get it out. The horses were caught and the cattle gathered up and pushed down on to the flat land. No sooner had they left the foothills than a truck came bouncing across the desert towards them. It was from the Bureau of Land Management.

"Hello Wes," Wes was greeted from the pickup as he sat his horse.

"Merl, how ya doing?" Wes answered.

"Fine, fine, Wes I hate to have to tell you this but I've been instructed to tell you that you can't pasture B.L.M. ground during the summer. I understand your situation with the Forest Service and I'm sorry, but there is nothing else I can do. Your grazing permits are for the winter months only."

"I'm not planning to graze, I'm just passing through," Wes explained.

"I know Wes, but cattle eat every chance they get. If it was up to me I'd say go ahead but if I let you through I could lose my job. I know you are a man of your word, Wes. Just tell me I won't see your cows on B.L.M. ground and I'll go away and leave you alone."

"You have my word," Wes told him.

Merl smiled at Nicole and Amy, hoping that they understood his awkward position, then said goodbye to Wes and drove away. Wes instructed them to push the cattle back a few hundred yards to the pond that the creek emptied into.

"This is Forest Service ground, that is B.L.M. ground," Wes pointed out the boundaries.

"The government sure owns a lot of ground around here," Nicole observed.

"Eighty-seven percent of the state," It was Amy that answered with a bitter edge to her voice.

"What are we going to do now?" Richard asked.

"Go see if we can get the truck out," Wes told him. "Amy will you stay and watch the cattle?"

She nodded.

"Nicole can help you."

"I think I should help get the truck out," Nicole informed him.

"As you please."

Arriving at the truck, Wes dismounted and walked around, surveying the situation.

"Lead the horses over the creek out of the way," Wes instructed Nicole. He got into the truck and maneuvered this way and that until it was cross ways in the narrow steep ground between the ridge and the creek bed. He could go neither forward nor backward.

"Wes, if we unhook the trailer we could go between these trees and those rocks. See that break in the trees over there? We could drive through there and get back in the track and back down here between that big tree and that stump and hook the trailer up from the side. We could then pull straight down the road."

"Alright, let's try it."

Soon Wes had the pickup backing towards

the trailer.

"Hold it!" Richard hollered.

"What's the matter?"

"The hitch on the trailer is a half Inch too, low. It won't go over the ball and you need to come back at a different angle or you'll hit that stump."

"O.K. Crank the trailer up a little and I'll come in at a different angle."

"It's cranked up as high as it'll go. The ground is higher here and I can't lift the trailer by myself," Richard informed Wes.

"I'll help lift. Nick, come and drive the truck for us. Now," Wes instructed her, "back up to here, then turn your wheels to the right, keep an eye on me and I'll guide you in from there."

Nicole got into the truck and began backing. She could see that she had to get the rear end to the left so she turned the wheels to make the front end of the truck move to the right.

"Hold it!" Wes yelled.

"What's the matter?"

"Turn to the right like I told you."

"I did."

"No you didn't! Pull up and try again!"

Nicole pulled up, jammed the gear shift back into reverse and started back.

"Turn!" Wes hollered.

Once again Nicole turned to make the, front end of the truck go right.

"Stop!" Wes yelled at her again, but this time it was too late as a sickening crunch accompanied by a stiff jolt brought her to a stop. She got out and walked around the truck to survey the damage. The stump was embedded in the right door.

"If you had turned your wheels the other way the front end would have swung away from the stump," Wes pointed out the obvious to her as if he was explaining something to a child.

"I know how to drive!" Nicole flared. "If you had told me the stump was there I wouldn't have run over it!"

"And what is wrong with obeying a simple request!?" Wes countered.

Nicole sucked in the necessary air for a forceful retort but Wes had turned and walked away, muttering to Richard something about a high fluting woman would rather freeze than follow a sensible suggestion from a stupid cowboy. Wes got into the pick up, drove forward a few feet, and then backed it within a few inches of the trailer.

"Now," Wes instructed her again, "when you see us lift the tongue of the trailer you back up carefully until you see us drop it on the ball, O.K.?" Wes was struggling to be civil.

Nicole got into the truck and waited while she looked through the rear window. The men strained and the tongue rose slowly until it was high enough. Nicole had a little trouble getting the truck in gear but by the time she backed up, the men had weakened and the tongue had sunk a fraction causing the hitch to knock the trailer back a few inches. The men would have to lift it even higher to hook it up. Nicole saw Wes place his hand over his eyes and draw it down over his face

"Let's try it again. You got it in gear?" Wes asked tiredly. Nicole nodded.

The cords in their arms and necks stood out with the effort but the tongue of the trailer rose to the desired height. The men let it down on the ball with a bang and stuck out their arms in defense as Nicole backed under the tongue with a jerk. With the trailer firmly hitched, Wes tried to maneuver truck and trailer down the track, but the angle was too great to get by the big tree without scraping the paint off all along side the trailer. No one spoke on the way back down to the pond.

They ate lunch and sat around the campfire, dozing in the sun. Occasionally, on a rotation basis someone had to ride out around the cattle to keep them from straying too far. At five o'clock sharp, Wes stood up from what Nicole had thought was a deep sleep and declared it was time to break camp. Quickly everything was packed and made ready to go. By five thirty they were mounted and instructed to push the cattle east across the B.L.M. land toward a wide swell.

"I thought you gave your word to Merl," Nicole was still irritated at Wes. Her resentment had grown during the day as she told herself how she had sacrificed her time and the money she would have earned to come and help, but did she get any thanks? NO! So what if she had made a few insignificant mistakes, did he acknowledge her unselfish intent? No! Did he appreciate the fact that she had ridden until her butt and her legs were sore, did he appreciate the fact that she had spent a cold, sleepless night on the hard ground; did he realize that he ordered her around like any other cow hand but that he wasn't paying her a nickel? No!

"I promised him he wouldn't see me," Wes was explaining when Nicole finished roasting him in her mind.

"If he forbade me to cross and I sneak across anyway without him knowing, he probably won't get into trouble."

"That sounds very deceptive to me," Nicole criticized.

"Are you a religious woman? I understand you go to church."

"Yes, I go to church."

"Do you believe the bible?"

"I do."

"What do you think of old father Abraham lying about his pretty little wife, Sarah to keep Pharaoh from killing him to get her? You do remember the story don't you?"

"Certainly. It's not the same."

"Why not?"

"Abraham was a prophet, a righteous man, he was doing what the Lord wanted him to."

"And I'm a wicked man and the Lord doesn't want anything to do with me?"

Wes was studying her face making her

nervous. She couldn't think of an answer that she could say out loud. Wes rode away and Richard moved his horse closer.

"It's impossible to argue with Wes," Richard told her. "One time I got mad and told him I hated his guts."

"What did he do?"

"He said I was entitled to my opinion but that I would respectfully keep it to myself or he'd throw my ass out of his house."

Nicole laughed despite herself.

"It's always funny to watch ol' Wes tangle with someone else but it's not so fun to be the one he starts on is it?" Richard said his piece and rode away.

Chapter Eleven

By six o'clock, the herd of cattle was moving steadily down the bottom of the wide swell. To an observer from a half a mile away it would have appeared as if the earth had opened up and swallowed the animals. Angling to the south east this swell continued to widen as it led across the high mesa and dropped into the valley through the low, flat topped hills rimming the valley on the west. Wes called a halt while the cattle were still between the low hills to see the colorful sunset.

"Wes doesn't strike me as the artistic type," Nicole was still smarting from her earlier encounter with him.

"He is waiting for darkness to push the cattle out into the open valley," Amy responded neutrally not knowing what Nicole's comment was meant to convey.

"He rushed us down here to sit and wait?"

"He didn't want to come down the draw in the dark. It's easy work in the daylight but can be treacherous at night. He wanted to wait until after Merl was off duty at five before starting. Once out of the hills we will turn south and angle across the valley. We should be off B.L.M. land by day light."

"Daylight? That's ten hours away!"

"If it's too much for you, ninety minutes straight east will put you in town," Amy issued the challenge.

"Why don't we drive the cattle to town and haul them out to Wes' at leisure?"

"The ranchers own this property all along this side of the valley. Many of them think that Wes is causing problems for them with the government agencies and would not allow him to cross their property under these circumstances. Wes has told them in pretty blunt terms that they are fools and that if things continue as they are little by little the ranchers will be pushed off all federal lards and be forced out of business. The first rancher that owns property along Federal ground that agrees with Wes is ten miles to the south. I'd guess that's where we are heading."

"You are only guessing?" Nicole asked hopefully.

"I'm pretty confident I'm right. I've been in the middle of this thing for years. My father ran a large herd of cattle on government lands but carried large debts. He thought he could negotiate with these people but they politely crowded him a little here and a little there, a little compromise here, another there, until they nibbled up his profit margin and he had to declare bankruptcy. He has a couple hundred acres of farm ground and pastures and a few head of cattle but he drives a school bus to feed his family. He still thinks that you can negotiate with these people if you just know what you're doing."

"What do you think, is Wes' way better?"

"I know Dad's way won't work. Wes' way may not either but he will force them to bare their naked fist. Maybe it will serve as a warning to others. It looks like it's time too move out. Are you going with us?"

"Of course!" Nicole was insulted.

The light had faded until one couldn't see for any distance and soon it was pitch black. Luckily the ground was more even with little vegetation to hide or mistake for a cow. The pace picked up once the moon came up. Many a time during the night Nicole wished she had taken Amy's suggestion and gone straight to town. Feeling like a reeling zombie by the time they had reached the friendly ranchers gate, Nicole was sure she was contributing nothing to the cattle drive.

"Amy, would you ride down and tell Grim what the situation is. Tell him we are going to push our cattle onto his property and tell him what the situation is and ask him if there is a place I can hold them until I can ship them home."

Amy rode briskly away. It was no easy trick herding the cattle through the gate in the faint glow of the dawn but by the time this was done Amy had returned with Grim.

"I didn't mean to get you up, Grim," Wes apologized.

"That's alright, that's alright!" Grim beamed, flashing the biggest, whitest smile Nicole had ever seen. She had seen him in town and at the bank and knew him to be one of the jolliest men she had ever met. The name on his bank account was Ronald Grimaldo.

"Feds ran you off eh?" Grim smiled.

"I had to sneak my cattle through in the night."

"Dirty bastards!" Grim cried vehemently, the smile never changing.

"Can you spare me some pasture or feed for a couple of days?"

"Sure, Wes, sure."

"You'll send me a bill," Wes stated.

"Go to hell you insulting son of a bitch," Grim beamed.

"Thanks, Grim," Nicole could see that Wes was touched by this show of friendship.

"Leave your rig in the hills?" Grim guessed.

"I'll give you a ride. Leave your horses here. You'll need them to work your cattle."

The saddles were stripped off the horses and thrown in the back of Grim's pickup. The three big men sat in the front seat of the cab while Amy and Nicole sat in the tiny back seat of Grim's king cab. Unlike Wes and Richard, Grim wasn't big and tall but big and wide and he liked to talk. The deep hum of his voice lulled Nicole until she dozed and started awake with each turn in the road. After an eternity of being teased with the much needed and desired sleep, they finally reached Wes' pickup. Once seated next to Wes on the return trip, Nicole abandoned every pretense and laid her head on him and promptly went to sleep. More than an hour had passed but at last they parked Wes' rig in front of his house.

"Richard, I think you all had better come in and get some sleep before you drive back. Show the girls to a room and pick one for yourself. We'll have a big breakfast when we wake up. I've got to make some phone calls right away.

Wes slide out from under Nicole's a head and propped her up and strode toward the door.

"Wake up, Nick," Amy nudged her. "Come on, dear." Amy urged her to slide out the door. Nicole groaned in pain as she slide out of the truck and put her weight on her stiff, raw legs.

"Here, let me help you," Amy put her arm around Nicole but Nicole pushed her away.

"I can make it," Trying not to show how painful it was to walk, Nicole moved slowly and stiffly into the house and laid down face first or the couch.

Amy headed straight for the shower Richard straight to bed. Hearing Amy emerge a few minutes later Nicole went into the bathroom and shut the door. Very carefully she undid her Levis and began to slide them down but they seemed to be stuck to her skin on the backs of her legs. She managed to pull them down two inches but the pain was too great. She gripped the side of the sink and tried not to make any noise as she wept and sniffled.

"Nick? Is something wrong?" Amy's concerned voice came through the door.

"No, I'm alright," she sobbed.

The door opened and Amy moved into the room dressed in a huge pair of pajama's and looked so clean and cute, not at all like she had been riding almost continuously for two days and a night.

"Tell me what's wrong, honey," Amy urged.

"My pants seem to be stuck to my legs."

"Let me see what's wrong," Amy gently tugged Nicole's Levis down to reveal the top of her legs. Nicole gasped with pain.

"Oh, I'm sorry!" Amy apologized. "I better tell Wes."

"NO!" Nicole almost shouted. "No, I'd rather you didn't," she added calmly. "Just ease them off, please."

Amy as carefully as she could eased Nicole's pants down two more inches. Nicole gripped the sink and cried silently.

"I'm sorry!"

The Levis came down two more inches. Nicole groaned.

"I'm sorry!"

"I don't think I can stand this," Nicole sobbed.

"Me either," Amy confessed, jerking Nicole's pants to her ankles. Nicole cried out in pain.

"I'm sorry!"

"Don't be. That was the most merciful way." Nicole stepped out of her Levis and turned to find Amy's face streaked with tears also.

"Your skin is rubbed raw. I suspect the plasma soaked into the material and then dried. You poor thing. You should have said something. You didn't have to go through this. Wes would have understood."

"No he wouldn't. All he thinks about is his precious cows," Nicole wailed. She calmed herself, then asked. "Will you do my panties? They are stuck too."

Amy's face scrunched up at the anticipated pain as if it was to be her own. Her tears began to flow more heavily but she nodded her head. Nicole turned back and gripped the sink and scrunched up her own face against the pain.

"What's that?" Amy stood still, listening intently.

Nicole strained to hear what Amy had heard. She then yelped in pain as Amy finished the job.

"I'm sorry!" Amy cried.

The water from the shower stung Nicole's raw skin at first but the pain gradually subsided, allowing her to wash her hair and emerge clean. She felt better. Amy carefully patted her dry for she found that it was painful to bend her legs. Amy had scrounged up an old robe of Wes' which she wrapped her in and led her to bed. Nicole lay down on her face and Amy covered her and fussed around her like she was a child, tucking and patting, her voice soft and reassuring.

"There, how does that feel?"

"Better. Thanks, Amy," Nicole's voice was already slurred with sleep.

Hours later Nicole awakened, disoriented in the darkening room. The stiffness and soreness reminded her where she was. She had slept all day, it now was dusk.

"Who's there?" She asked groggily as she sensed someone in the room.

"It's me," Amy's voice came softly. "I didn't mean to wake you. Wes suggested that I spread same Aloe Vera gel on your legs and bottom. He said it's very healing for burns and thought it might help. You wanna try it?"

Nicole intended to refuse but as she tried to roll over she found that she was so sore she couldn't bend. She fell back onto her stomach.

"Anything to get out of here," she mumbled.

Amy pulled back the blankets and drew up Nicole's robe.

"Oh, you poor dear," her voice full of sympathy.

With a paring knife, Amy slit the fat spears of the Aloe Vera and flattened it out exposing the clear sticky gel. This she placed on Nicole' rear. Nicole jerked and gasped.

"I'm sorry!" Amy cried.

"It didn't hurt,' Nicole assured her, "but it's cold."

Amy continued slitting the spears and covering the raw areas with the gel.

"There, all done."

"Thank goodness. I'm freezing and it tickled so bad I could hardly stand it. That was very soothing. Thank you."

"Wes is going to bring you in some supper. Richard and I will be leaving. I'm sure you will be all right."

Nicole found that she didn't want Amy to leave her in her predicament. She, in her need, had found the younger woman to be a sensitive and caring nurse but she was sure Amy wouldn't understand her reluctance to have to rely on Wes' personal attention.

"You've been very kind to me. I won't forget it," Nicole said feelingly.

"Weren't nothing." Amy waved her hand.

"Gotta run, Richard is waiting."

Nicole could hear Wes thanking Amy and Richard for their help.

"If Richard is so foolish as to ever let you get away, I'd like to hire you as my foreman. I couldn't have done without you, sweetheart. I appreciate your help too, son," Wes' voice was as casual and normal as always but this was the first time Nicole had ever heard him call Richard 'son'.

"Glad to help, Wes," Richard was embarrassed. "Let's go, Amy."

A few minutes later Wes entered and switched on the light. He was carrying a tray of food. It smelled wonderful and tasted delicious, she didn't stop until she was stuffed; Wes cheerfully visited with her the whole time but she paid him little attention and resented his cheerfulness.

"Thank you, Wes," Nicole was polite. "I'm tired, Wes, would you mind if I went back to sleep?" Nicole said to get rid of him.

"No, no, I don't mind. See you in the morning." He turned out the light and left.

Not surprisingly, Nicole found that she was as tired as she had led Wes to believe. She quickly drifted off to sleep and didn't awaken until after sun up the next morning. On the nightstand was a tray with freshly cut Aloe Vera, and on the foot of the bed lay her freshly washed clothes. She doctored herself, dressed and left her room in search of Wes but the house was empty. She found food lain out for breakfast which she cooked and ate, still no Wes. She went out to the veranda and looked towards the sheds and corrals but couldn't see him. Then she noticed his truck and trailer were missing. She hung around the house until mid-morning, telling herself it was impolite to leave without speaking to her host, but finally gave it up and walked to her car, got in, backed around and started down the road.

She hadn't gone far when she saw dust in the distance. As the vehicle drew closer, she could see that it was Wes. She slowed and pulled over to the side of the road. He too pulled over and stopped indicating he wanted to talk. His trailer was full of cows and calves that he must have been hauling from Grim's.

"Hello, Nick. I see you're up and about today. You gonna to be O.K.?"

"I'll be fine."

"You get something to eat?"

"Yes." Nicole could see that Wes knew she was irritated with him, but he didn't have a clue as to why. How could he be so thick headed?!

"Thanks for your help," Wes said awkwardly.

"I'm afraid I wasn't much help."

"You done real good for a tenderfoot," Wes tried to compliment, but Nicole equated 'tenderfoot' with incompetent, with the excuse of being new at a job. Nicole didn't consider herself a tenderfoot. After all, she had been riding two or three times a month for a year. She had gotten off on the wrong foot is all.

"I'm expected back," She drove off fuming.

She had calmed down forty minutes later as she pulled into town and stopped at the gas station.

"Would you fill it and check the oil and coolant for me, please?" she asked the attendant. With an amused look, the attendant put the nozzle in the tank and went to the rear and put up the hood.

"The oil is fine," he told her as he stood once more at her window.

"And the coolant?"

The look of amusement intensified.

"You just buy this car from Wes?" the attendant asked.

"Yes. Is there something wrong?"

"Not a thing, but there is no coolant. This has an air cooled engine," Seeing that Nicole didn't understand, he continued to explain.

"A water cooled engine has a radiator through which liquid circulates and is cooled by the fan. The coolant then runs through the engine and cools it, see?"

"Yes, I know about that."

"But an engine that is air cooled doesn't have a radiator per say, but, the oil itself runs through small tubes or fins similar to those in a radiator. The oil is cooled by a fan and then circulates back through the engine cooling it, understand?" The attendant was laughing at her, much to her embarrassment. She could have coped with not understanding the mechanics of a Volkswagen but now the whole town would know Wes had made a fool of her. Back in her little, barren, lonely house she cursed Wes and vowed she would have nothing more to do with him. She would eradicate his memory from her mind. She would go back to school and get her degree.

She returned to work the following day, wearing a loose fitting dress. Although Wes' treatment had greatly relieved her discomfort, she was still stiff and sore. She had planned to give Mr. Trimble notice that she was planning to quit, but the day passed without the opportunity presenting itself.

That evening after work, she was pleasantly surprised to discover a note from her mother in the mall box. She was stunned to learn that her mother was requesting the pleasure of her company at her wedding taking place only six days in the future.

Nicole felt like a stranger sitting in her mother's house during the wedding and afterwards at the wedding party. Her mother with the color of high excitement on her cheeks was nearly as giddy as any young bride and treated her more like a guest than a daughter. Only a few intimate friends had been invited with Wes conspicuously absent. Nicole was irritated at her mother after all that Wes had done to help them, but she said nothing for there existed the distant possibility that Wes had been invited but had chosen not to come.

Nicole hugged and kissed her mother and wished her and Roark a happy life together. On the drive back to town the realization came that never again would she fit in as a member of her mother's household. Only a short stay would be acceptable to either herself or her mother. The week at work dragged slowly by but not as slowly as her time alone at home in the evenings. The few eligible young men of the valley had given up asking her out. First her time had been taken up by Richard, and later she had kept her time free in case Wes called her. For the umpteenth time she resolved to talk to Mr. Trimble and give him notice, but now it would have to wait until Monday.

Sunday morning after she had showered, dressed and sat combing out her hair, she was startled by a knock on the door! Someone had actually come to see her.

"Morning, Nick," Wes stood twirling his hat in his hand.

"Get your cows fed already?" Nicole asked sweetly.

"Yeah, they're fed. I started early. I come by to take you to breakfast if I may," Wes invited.

"I've had breakfast and I'm getting ready for church."

"Oh." Wes twirled his hat some more. "I could give you a lift," he suggested with sudden inspiration.

"I like to walk when the weather is so nice."

"Look, Nick, I consider you a good and faithful friend. All I ask is the chance to make up for what I've done."

A good and faithful friend wasn't all that Nicole wanted to be, but she relented.

"Alright, you may go to church with me."

This was more than Wes had bargained for and he hesitated, looking down at his boots and Levis but he agreed. Forty five minutes later, Wes led her into the church and found them a seat in the back pew. Not long into the sermon Wes began to snore loud enough to cause the people in front to turn and look, but when Nicole was about to nudge him, she noticed that Wes' eyes were open and his expression normal. However, the lady in front of them jerked her head up at the sound. She had been asleep and everyone thought that it was she who had been snoring. It wasn't long before the lady's head began to nod but no sooner than she did, Wes began to snore. Once again her head jerked up only to find the people looking at her, some in irritation, others with delighted smiles on their faces. With her head twisted a little to one side, she hissed quietly at Wes,

"Lionel, you cut that out!"

The sermon droned on and on, seducing the poor woman until her head drooped once more. Wes snored.

"Damned you, Lionel!"

Nicole got the giggles and had to bow her head and cover her mouth to keep from embarrassing herself. Before the meeting was over, Wes got to perform one more time.

"Lionel!" The woman's voice was deadly.

Finally the meeting was over. Nicole was exhausted with the effort required to control her giggles. Wes sat stoically, through the whole episode. Wes led Nicole outside, but stopped her with a hand on her arm. He didn't speak but merely stood and waited. He didn't have long to wait. Wes' victim emerged, spotted him and made a beeline towards them. She was tall and slim, with dark hair streaked with gray. She was handsome and dignified but at the moment her dark eyes were snapping.

"Lionel Wesly, you are going straight to

hell! What on earth am I going to do with you!?
When are you ever going to grow up and show
some respect to..."

"Mother," Wes interrupted politely, "I
would like you to meet Nicole Defoe. She is the one
I told you about that did so much to help me save
my cattle. Nicole, this is my mother, Georgia
Wesly."

With one last angry look at Wes, Wes'
mother turned to Nicole, her expression changing
completely to one of interest.

"I'm very pleased to meet you, dear."

Wes persuaded the ladies to take lunch with
him by telling his mother that Richard was to meet
them at the cafe to see his grandmother. Georgia
then insisted that Nicole join them and she was a
very hard person to say no to. They were seated by
the time Richard showed up.

"I thought Amy was coming with you?" Wes
looked disappointed.

"She is mad at me," Richard confessed.

"What did you do to her?" Wes asked
critically.

"Nothing, honest, Wes."

"What were you saying when she got mad?"

Richard glanced anxiously at Nicole then
motioned Wes to follow him. The two men walked
to the back of the room in the corner, away from all
other customers where Richard turned his back
towards them. Wes followed suit.

"This sun is too hot, shining through the window like that," Georgia declared. "Let's move." She chose a booth that suited her. Nicole realized that they were sitting with their backs to the two men and couldn't be seen but they could hear clearly. Georgia sat perfectly quiet with no pretense of making conversation and when Nicole glanced at her she winked and said. "I hate being left out don't you?"

"Wes, you know a lot about women," Richard was saying, "I haven't been doing too well here in the valley recently. Could you give me some insight on how to understand 'em?"

"Sure, I know a lot about women but so do you. I don't pretend to understand 'em. There is one thing I know, if she's mad, apologize."

"But I don't know why she is mad!" Richard protested.

"Don't make no difference, just make sure you are vague so you don't apologize for the wrong thing, and then do something nice for her like take her to dinner or send her a flower. But make sure she knows you bought it and not just picked it."

"Why?"

"I don't know. That's just how it is."

Nicole understood then that Wes had been following his own advice that very morning. She had to acknowledge it worked. She had all ready forgiven him, to a degree, and even learning that he was still ignorant of the source of her anger, his attempts to make amends were touching.

"Tell me what you were saying when she got mad and maybe I can help," Wes offered.

"I ah ..was hugging her and kissing her a little... ya know? And she was getting ... ah... a little ... ah excited...ya know? And...ah...."

"Alright, you had her turned on. What did you say?"

"I told her she was number one with me. That's all Wes and she got mad," Richard was dismayed.

"You didn't? You bone head!"

"What's wrong with that?"

"What's wrong with that? I'll tell, you what's wrong with that. To say that she is number one implies that there is a number two and three or more... She knows as well as I do that there are three in this valley let alone what you may have up in Reno."

"You are behind the times, Wes. Those other two are history."

"And the ones in Reno? Just as I thought," Wes added when Richard didn't answer. "Look, maybe it's all right for them sophisticated city women to be number one but down here when a woman falls in love with a guy she wants to be 'one and only,' not 'number one.' Get it?"

"That's all she is mad at?"

"Look, Richard that is one tough, smart, little gal as you well know. What you may not know is that she is very tender hearted. If you're not willing to be 'one and only' for her, may I suggest you show enough back bone to move on and leave her alone. She'll be hurt plenty as it is. I tell you son, if I were fifteen..., if I were twenty years younger I'd make a run at her myself."

The two men almost walked right by the two women but stopped short with worried expressions on their faces. Each searched his own mind to see if he had said something that he might regret.

"We found the sun too hot," Georgia smiled.

Lunch was ordered and served a short time later. Georgia carried the conversation, giving most of her attention to Richard. She talked knowledgeably about many subjects. She was well traveled and well read, a woman of refinement and culture.

"Wes, I hate to bring this up, we're having such a nice time, but since we are all here together I think is for the best." Georgia smiled a little sadly.

Wes looked apprehensive.

"I must confess that I have been foolish, I have lived a little beyond my means and with unexpected business reverses I find myself with the necessity of looking for a job. I'm not retirement age for three more years." As she talked her face gradually settled into an expression of disbelief and hurt.

"Gloria won't let me come and live with her and Caroline says she is in the middle of a home remodel. I don't have anywhere else to land. It won't be for long Wes, only for a couple of years," Georgia was almost pleading.

Nicole and Richard were embarrassed at her
need to talk to her son in this manner.

"Can we talk about it later, Mother?' Wes
suggested uneasily.

"I think that we should hear what Richard
and Nicole have to say since we will all be living
under the same roof," Georgia insisted.

"What're you talking about?" Wes asked
suspiciously.

"Didn't you write and tell me Richard was
staying with you?"

"He's moved out."

"Well you didn't tell me that. But there is
still your, what shall we call it, arrangement or
understanding with Nicole." Noticing the look on
Nicole's face Georgia quickly apologized.

"I'm terribly sorry. I can see he hasn't
mentioned it to you yet."

"That's enough, mother!" Wes' deeply
tanned skin darkened even more.

Georgia's face was the epitome of rejection
and sorrow.

"Maybe Gloria will let me sleep in her
garage until she gets her house finished."

"You said it was Caroline that was
remodeling," Wes corrected.

Georgia waved her hand to indicate Wes
was being picky over something insignificant.

"We had some good times together," she
continued as if the relationship was over.

208

"Remember that time I came here for Thanksgiving when Richard was just a tyke? You were still living in that little trailer with Stephanie. She had the cutest little napkins with turkeys on them. Richard kept following me around all day trying to get the turkey on his napkin to do something. He got the strangest idea from somewhere."

"I remember his grandmother jerking her napkin away from her lips and crying, 'That damned turkey kicked me!' That's what I remember."

"I did not. You have me mixed up with someone else."

Lunch was over as they sat and waited for Georgia to carefully reapply her lipstick. It was done so perfectly that Nicole was surprised when she blotted her lips on a napkin and she left the perfect job quite smeared. While waiting for Wes to pay the bill, Georgia exclaimed.

"Oh Richard, you have food around your mouth." Georgia reached up and wiped his mouth for him.

"I used to have to do this for him when he was little," Georgia explained to Nicole.

"Thanks for lunch, Wes. I gotta run." But as Richard started past, Georgia took him by the arm and turned him around toward the cashier.

"Don't forget to come and see me you young rascal," she purred.

The cashier looked at Richard with eyebrows raised in mild shock, for his mouth was smeared with Georgia's lipstick. Seeing her expression Richard explained.

"Linda, this is my grandmother."

The look of shock deepened but Linda was unable to respond. Richard shrugged and left.

Chapter 12

During lunchtime on Monday, Nicole walked dawn to the cafe to eat and ran into a morose Wes.

"Hello Wes, why so glum?"

"I'm missing twenty-four cows and their calves. On top of that Jules has filed suit against me and we have charged him with the felony of cattle rustling. I'm tired of it all."

Wes had known all this yesterday at the cafe but it hadn't seemed to bother him then Nicole thought. It must be something else.

"How's your mother?"

"Happy as a lark," Wes' depression deepened visibly.

Nicole knew she had found the real source of Wes' depression.

"I really liked your mother. She obviously is a woman of great ability and confidence even though you wouldn't suspect she had such a sense of humor, she is so refined."

"She's a fine actress you mean."

"Wes! Don't you like your mother? I thought you were rude to her yesterday. I've never seen you treat anyone like that before and I was disappointed in you," Nicole stated firmly.

"Nicole," Wes began patiently, "that crack she made yesterday about you and I having an arrangement was said out of pure malice. I never told her any such thing."

"I can't believe she would do that for no good reason," Nicole defended.

"Revenge."

"Revenge?"

"Revenge," Wes emphasized. "She was mad because I snored behind her at church."

"What did Richard do to her?"

"Nothin', that trick she pulled on him was just for fun. I don't know where she comes up with all that nonsense. She better be careful carrying on like that at her age, they'll put her in the nut house," Wes was disgusted.

Nicole began to laugh. Richard reacted to Wes' antics the same as Wes reacted to his mother's.

"What's so funny?"

"Nothing," Nicole smiled fondly it him.

Three times that week Nicole found Wes at the cafe seeking solace from her in regards to his house guest. Each day he looked gloomier and on Sunday, for the first time ever, Nicole saw Wes in a suit with his hair slicked back. He was sitting straight backed and miserable next to his mother on the front pew of the church. He looked grateful when Nicole slid in next to him. Once again the three of them met Richard at the café for lunch after the services. Once again Richard showed up alone.

"Still mad?" Wes asked.

Richard nodded, his mood matching Wes' own.

"You didn't do what I told you to," Wes asserted.

"Yes I did. But you can imagine how successful I was with lipstick smeared all over my face," Richard looked daggers at his grandmother.

"Serves you right, you were being mean to her," Georgia defended.

"I wasn't either!" Richard protested.

Conversation over lunch reminded Nicole of skillfully, well fought, fencing match with Georgia against her two descendants. Surprisingly, it was done with little real passion but with considerable enthusiasm. At first it was a real strain on Nicole who was used to a much less aggressive environment but after a while she was able to relax and enjoy herself.

The only relapse Georgia had they were once again standing in front of Linda as Wes paid the check.

"You didn't come and see me Sweetheart," she chided Richard as she pinched him playfully on the cheek.

Richard flushed and pulled away.

Business at the bank Tuesday morning was slow when Nicole looked up to see Amy standing at her window. Her eyes were bright with excitement, accompanied by a not quite suppressed smile, but she only asked politely to have a check cashed. As Nicole turned to count out the money, she noticed that Amy had casually but carefully placed her hand flat on the counter between them. The big stone flashed it's brilliance in the morning sun.

"Amy!" Nicole cried. "It's beautiful!" She picked up Amy's hand to examine the ring. She had recognized it immediately although it had been resized to fit Amy's smaller, daintier finger. Amy was beaming with happiness and pride.

"Surprised?"

"Yes I am. Oh, not that he'd propose to you," Nicole quickly amended, "but the last I heard you two weren't getting along too well."

"Georgia Wesly came to see me," Amy explained. "She told me about the little trick she, played on Richard just to help straighten him out a little bit. She was so sweet and helpful. I wish I had a grandmother like that."

"She is nice, isn't she," Nicole agreed.

Amy looked almost furtively around the bank, but seeing that it was empty except for Turnbill sitting back in his office, she lowered her voice and spoke confidentially.

"Georgia suggested that I tell you a bit of information, seeing as how you are interested in Wes and all, and might one day need to know this." Again Amy's eyes darted about the roam to make certain no one was there. There wasn't, but her voice dropped even lower.

"She told me that in the Wesly family there

is a tradition that they never circumcise the baby boys. She read the part in the bible where it says you can still be a good Christian and not be. Did you know that some of the greatest men weren't? There was Thomas Jefferson, Ulysses S. Grant, and Casanova. She said this explained a lot."

"What?" Nicole wondered.

"Why some men are so aggressive as leaders and in their private lives, ya know? She wanted us to understand why Richard and maybe Wes would need so much, ah, personal attention that way, ya know? She doesn't really know if they were, I mean weren't, but she didn't want us to be surprised."

"Thank you for sharing that, it might be very helpful to know."

"Well, I wanted you to be the first to know that we are engaged. We've been through SO much together, with Wes and Richard. Oh!" Amy exclaimed as a new thought came to her. "Please don't think I came to gloat. I've come to admire you and I want to be your friend, especially if you and Wes... Georgia said Wes has his eye on .... Wouldn't it be great if we were in the same...?"

Seeing Nicole's expression, Amy's voice trailed off in confusion. Nicole couldn't help but worry that Richard might become embarrassed by his pretty little unsophisticated, guileless country wife, the same as Sophi had become ashamed of Wes. Amy would make the perfect wife for Wes, but of course there was twenty something years difference in their ages that would be too great for

Amy to consider. Why was everybody always falling in love with the wrong people?

"You are just what Richard needs. I hope you will be very happy," Nicole said with tears coming to her eyes. "I want so badly for you to stay and live in the valley."

"Oh, thank you!" Amy responded with tears of her own. Nicole squeezed Amy's hand and would have hugged her but for the counter between them. Amy left, smiling though her tears.

The week went by without Nicole seeing hide nor hair of Wes. Her wrath had been blunted sufficiently to allow her to realize that she still wanted him but her hopes were fading, not withstanding Georgia's rumor mill. Irritated at herself for looking forward to church, in hopes that Georgia would once again prevail upon her son to attend, Nicole entered the building glancing left and right. Sure enough, right there in front was the Wesly family but this time, Richard sat stiff, combed and miserable in his new suit next to Amy.

Amy spotted her and motioned Nicole over, making room next to Wes. Stifling her pride, Nicole took her seat. Once again Georgia invited everyone to lunch at the cafe. Much to Nicole's surprise Wes was in a jovial mood, laughing and joking and bantering with his mother. He actually was enjoying the mental exercise required to keep up with her. When Wes wasn't looking, Nicole saw Georgia looking at him with speculation, even suspicion.

"Did you ever find your missing cows?" Nicole asked.

"Nope. The sheriff thinks that someone picked them up at the same time the Forest Service was gathering them. They ran them over into California. I guess they were hoping that I would blame the Forest Service and they would get away clean."

"What were they worth?"

"Well the price is always fluctuating, but they would be worth in the neighborhood of sixteen thousand." Wes' spirits were dampened for a time by the thoughts of his loss but soon he was sparring with his mother once again. So it wasn't that, Nicole thought. Richard and Amy didn't have much to say as they held hands under the table and were content to watch the show. Georgia didn't do anything to embarrass Richard this time. Nicole hung back while Wes paid the check as the others went outside.

"You are sure in a good mood today," Nicole probed.

"Mother's leaving," Wes stated happily.

"But don't say anything. She doesn't know it yet. I did some checking and found out she hasn't lost a dime of her fortune. She is as rich and spoiled as ever. She is staying just to teach me a lesson."

"You mean for snoring behind her in church? That's a little extreme, don't you think?"

"You don't know my mother," Wes

asserted.

Somehow that didn't sound right to Nicole. She would have to watch and discover the real reason.

"Nick," Wes was hesitant, "would you do me a big favor?"

"Sure, Wes."

"Would you drive out to the place after work on Tuesday?"

"Sure. What's going on?"

"Here's twenty five bucks for gas."

"I won't use that much, Wes!" Nicole protested.

"You might do a little more driving than you think. Take it. It's worth it to me."

"What are we going to do?"

"Never mind, just keep this to yourself."

Curiosity ate at Nicole for two days but finally the time came for her to drive out to Wes'. The day was lovely with the first tempering of the summer heat, as the days began to grow a bit shorter in the early fall. Her spirits rose as she tried to guess what Wes had in mind. Despite her best intentions, she found herself day dreaming of him taking her in his arms and declaring his love and desire for her. The memory of his hands gently caressing her shoulders and his clean manly sell mixed with his after shave lotion was always near, nibbling at the edges of her mind. She sighed wistfully, knowing full well that there was nothing in Wes' manner to lead her to expect any romantic exchange.

Georgia answered the door.

"Nicole! What a surprise! Come in dear." Georgia led Nicole back into the kitchen where she had been preparing supper. Although the table had been set for two, Georgia set another place, visiting pleasantly the whole time. Nicole quietly began helping and let her host direct her when needed.

"Poor Wes," Georgia was saying, "sitting out here all by himself with no one to consider but himself. He gets kind of sloppy in his housekeeping and I know he isn't eating like he should, and without the refining influence of a woman, I'm afraid he is getting rougher in his manners than ever before." Georgia looked pointedly at Nicole. Embarrassed by the blunt inference, Nicole looked away but then Georgia continued.

"It's a good thing I'm here to look after him."

Supper was ready and still no Wes.

"Why don't you relax for a few minutes, dear? If Wes doesn't show up, we will eat without him. He works so hard, sometimes he forgets to come home on time," Georgia apologized for Wes. .

For a time Nicole sat alone in Wes' den, a room she liked, but becoming bored, she got up and began puttering about looking at his things. The bookcase drew her attention as it had in times past. Pulling down the 'C' encyclopedia, she shuffled through the pages to the word circumcision. Her reading confirmed a suspicion that had been growing in the back of her mind. Georgia had fabricated another story. Nicole had also begun to suspect that some of Georgia's stories were told with an ulterior motive, even if she did have a great time telling them. Was this particular one told to make the Wesly men seem more mysterious and attractive to Amy and herself?

Georgia came in and suggested that they eat.

"There is no reason for everyone to eat a warmed over meal," she declared.

The meal was nearly consumed when the kitchen door banged open and in staggered Wes. His eyes were rolling back in his head and there was spittle drooling down his chin, a gagging choking sound came from his throat and it appeared as if he were trying to speak. Suddenly he collapsed, smashing the table and scattering the chairs as Georgia and Nicole leaped out of the way. Georgia was the first to recover.

"Call 911!" she screamed.

"No time," Wes groaned from the floor.

"Juice, diabetes," he finished in a whisper.

Comprehension flooded Nicole's mind and in an instant she was pouring orange juice into a glass and bending and holding it to Wes' lips. Swallow by swallow she coaxed it down him. Slowly Wes' eyes lost their wild gyrations and his breathing evened out. "Diabenies pills...left bottom shelf...cupboard," he finally managed.

Georgia quickly moved to the cupboard and began frantically searching.

"Here it is," she said with forced control.

"It's empty!" her control vanished and she began wringing her hands and crying.

"Gotta have insulin. Doc Blake at the clinic," Wes whispered feebly.

With great effort, the two frightened women wrestled Wes out to the truck only to find that the keys weren't in their usual place in the ignition. They propped him up and coaxed him to walk to Nicole's V.W., which he did on tottering legs. Seeing that he probably couldn't sit up, Nicole pulled the back seat forward and guided him onto the back seat as he lost his balance and nose dived in. The two women wrestled his legs in and draped them over the back of the front seat that lay forward, and slammed the door.

"Go!" Georgia waved Nicole away. "I'll call Blake and tell them you're coming!" Georgia was already making a beeline back to the house before Nicole had the car started. The little car fishtailed as it made the turn just before leaving the gravel road onto the blacktop.

"Careful. I'd like to live through this," Wes admonished her. Keeping her eyes glued to the road, Nicole drove as fast as she dared for the twenty five miles to town. She jerked up the emergency brake once she was in front of the clinic and bolted toward the door.

"I gotta see Doctor Blake!" she demanded of the receptionist.

The doctor, having heard the commotion Nicole had caused coming through the door, stuck his head out from the hallway.

"Wes' stuff is right there on the counter," he pointed.

"But…"

"Give it to him, he'll be alright," The doctor smiled and disappeared.

The receptionist handed Nicole a paper bag as Nicole turned. Nicole jerked the top open and saw a small box labeled insulin syringes and several small vials. She rushed these out to Wes who was sitting calmly in the front seat. Piqued she tossed these at him as she got in. She banged the door shut.

"You could have told me on the way in," she grated. "I'm supposed to be in on this, remember?"

"I had to make sure you were fooled or for sure mother wouldn't have been," Wes chuckled.

"What's in the vials?"

"Sugar water."

"What is it for?"

"Mother can't stand the sight of a needle, she faints every time she has to have a shot and of course she couldn't even think about giving someone else a shot. There is no one to doctor me unless I were to hire a nurse," Wes explained, smiling wickedly. "I'll have to have a special diet, very complicated of course, with snacks several times a day, not to mention the danger of blackouts and even death, quite a burden for a woman her age without any resources.

"How you and your mother can treat each other this way I'll never know. Don't you have any affection for her at all?" Nicole was aghast at Wes' plan.

"We love each other dearly but we can't get along worth beans. I don't know why, just one of those things," Wes shrugged. "It's better that she leaves so we can continue liking each other. Surely you can see it would never do for her to stay here any length of time."

Nicole had to concede this last point. Back at Wes' Nicole listened while Wes outlined duties to his mother. She listened carefully with tight nervous set to her mouth. He had her give him a shot in the hip right there on the front room couch with Nicole looking on.

"Ouch! Damn it, Mother," Wes complained loudly. "It's supposed to go in the hip not the cheek."

"Oh hush up, you big baby," she countered.

The three of them then went into the kitchen to clean up the mess. Wes muttered his displeasure at the situation the whole time. He complained about the cost of replacing the broken dinnerware, the high cost of the medicine that he would have to buy for the rest of his life, not to mention the loss of his cattle and the reduced time he could pasture government land. From there, he went on to how this new inconvenience would hamper his work, having to come back to the house so often to get his medicine.

Later that evening when Nicole left they were still at it. She had her doubts that Wes' plan was going to work but two days later, Georgia was on the phone asking her to ride up to Reno with them. She was going to catch a flight back home and she didn't want Wes driving around alone in his condition. Wes and his mother stopped by her little house in Wes' pickup. Georgia got out and indicated that, Nicole should get in and ride in the middle next to Wes.

"I tend to get car sick if I don't ride by the window," she said, looking Nicole right in the eye.

They arrived at the airport in Reno several hours later, tired and hungry but there was, no time to go out to eat.

"Don't worry about me, I'll get something on the plane," Georgia assured Wes. Having a few minutes before departure, Wes hurried off to find a rest room.

"I can't tell you how much I have enjoyed your visit," Nicole told her truthfully.

Georgia sighed, "I only wish I could stay a little longer, but it's probably best for you that I'm going. Wes hates to be pushed into anything and I can't help but push when I can see what would be so good for him." Georgia's direct gaze prohibited any denial on Nicole's part. Nicole nodded, acknowledging the truth.

"I'll look after him," Nicole promised.

"Nicole, I know full well Wes doesn't have

diabetes," Georgia laughed at Nicole's expression.

"After you left that day and I called the doctor, he seemed too casual for the situation. It occurred to me that a diabetic patient doesn't act the way Wes was acting. Wes kept recovering just enough to suggest what we should do. Even though it hurt me so badly to give him those shots I had to avoid letting him know that I had caught on. He would have been so disappointed. I found I couldn't do it one more time, he's such a wimp. Did you know that when he was a boy he used to faint every time he had to have a shot?"

Nicole listening to Georgia's explanation found herself believing that Wes got those shots as punishment for deceiving, his mother.

"Here are two tickets for a dinner show tonight." Georgia pressed these into Nicole's hand quickly for Wes was returning.

The call for Georgia's flight came over the intercom.

"Well, this is it, Wes," Georgia managed to look like a forlorn little girl being shipped away to boarding school against her will.

"Have a nice trip," Wes answered cheerfully.

"Don't worry about me, I don't want to be a burden on anyone, I'll be all right," Georgia's voice was full of self pity, her face long, but she squared her shoulders and gave Wes a motherly peck on the cheek and turned away. Wes let her get two strides away before, calling after her,

"Give my regards to Jason."

She stopped dead still, then turned slowly, a big smile pushing its way across her face.

"I love you, mother," Wes said tenderly.

"I love you too, son," her eyes glistening.

Once again she turned and walked away, but with head high and a bounce to her step.

"Who is Jason?" Nicole asked.

"Her present business manager," Wes grinned.

Nicole and Wes were seated near the stage as they watched a very entertaining show designed for families. Wes never touched alcohol, so Nicole drank the two glasses of champagne served as part of the meal to each adult diner. By the time the show was over she was feeling quite relaxed. She laughed too loudly at the antics of the performers and said a lot of silly things that she giggled at, thinking she was funny. When she stood up to go, she was unsteady on her feet. Wes took her arm and guided her out to the truck and opened the door for her. She felt light and comfortable as she sat leaning against the door while they drove away from the lights of the city into the desert. She watched his face as he smiled at her comments. Soon she became quiet.

"Damn he is, sexy!" she thought.

With an effort she slid carefully across the seat and snuggled up to him laying her head against his shoulder. He continued to talk to her as if she was still on the other side of the truck. She

226

unsnapped the front of his shirt and ran her hand across his chest. She was now feeling very sleepy and wanted to be cuddled.

"Wes?"

"Umm?"

"Do you think I'm sexy?" she murmured.

Three hours later she stirred. The pain in her neck and cramps in her legs penetrated the benumbed brain communicating to her the fact that she had been in a most uncomfortable position for a long time. She moved, sending pins and needles up and down her legs and one arm.

"Where am I?" she asked.

"We have just dropped off the desert into the valley."

She realized she was sprawled across the seat with her head bent against the seat and Wes' ribs. Painfully she sat up and looked owlishly around. The pleasant glow from the champagne had faded, leaving a slight head ache and upset stomach. Brushing at her hair with her fingers, she was painfully aware of the silent, nearly immobile man next to her, staring tiredly down the road. By the time she had stretched the cramps out of her muscles, the pickup was slowing in front of her house. Wes stopped the truck and pulled the handle of the door, causing the cab light to come on.

"Don't," Nicole commanded.

"Are you sure?" He turned back. Lipstick was smudged over his ear, cheek and neck.

"I can make it," she said dully, opening her

own door and sliding out. With head high and back straight, more for balance than anything else, she walked unsteadily inside, shutting the door and leaning back on it. Resting for a few minutes to gather her strength she pushed herself away and tottered into the bedroom. Mechanically she undressed and flopped into bed. Late the next morning she awoke with a rising panic, she was late for work! Slowly it came to her that it was Saturday. With a relieved sigh, she settled back onto the pillow.

Painfully the events of the previous night came crowding into her mind and for the first time the significance of Wes' lipstick smeared face connected with the brief glimpse she had seen of her own smeared face as she had passed the mirror on her way to bed.

It occurred to her that he had no lipstick on his lips. She must have wallowed her face against him for some time to paint him up like that. In her mind's eye she could see him patiently driving mile after mile with eyes on the road as a drunken woman feebly nuzzled and pawed him. She remembered asking him if he thought she was sexy but couldn't remember if he had answered. The image of her hand unsnapping his shirt front came forth vividly to accuse her. Wishing with an acute ache that she had never gone with him to Reno she began to weep. No way would she ever be able to face him again.

Correctly guessing that Wes would not go to church once his mother left, Nicole got ready and went by herself. She sat on the one side of Richard and Amy sat on the other. Nicole's mind wandered all during the sermon.

"Pay attention!" she scolded herself silently.

"For all you are learning today you may as well have stayed home. It did little good. Finally Nicole bowed head and went to sleep. Being started awake by a gentle shaking, Nicole looked sheepishly around. Amy was leaning across Richard as the other people were standing and leaving.

"Are you alright?" Amy's face was worried.

"Yes, I'm fine, just a little tired."

Chapter 13

As the days slipped by into weeks, Nicole's routine existence kept her moving in an incessant circle around a heart that was still alive but in a coma. It came as no surprise that the only time she saw Wes was a chance meeting at the grocery store. He had been friendly but had only asked after her well being like he would have done with any other neighbor. There had been nothing in his manner that even suggested that he was thinking about the trip home from Reno with her. For this she was grateful.

Saying that weddings were no fun anymore because people stood in a line and said "How are you?" and were answered "Fine thank you. How are you?" then they ate a sandwich I that wouldn't satisfy a mouse and they were expected to drive many miles to leave an expensive gift and turn around and drive home again, Amy decided to have an old fashioned wedding with a dance and dinner. Her father barbecued a full beef while the rest of the family and even some friends provided salads, rolls, cakes, and several specialty dishes. A live country and western band and a few simple decorations in the high school gym provided a good time for everyone in the valley.

"Amy," Nicole got the brides attention, "I

didn't think Richard would get you out of your boots long enough to get you to the preacher."

Grinning from ear to ear, the lovely little bride raised her long white dress a foot off the floor to reveal dainty high heeled white boots.

"Have you decided on a place to live?" Nicole asked her.

"We would like to stay here in the valley but we can't find anything to rent," Amy's disappointment plainly showed.

"Would my little house be big enough to start out in?"

"Yes ,but..."

"I'm giving notice to Mr. Trimble tomorrow. I'm moving up to Reno. I will be out before you get back from your honeymoon. The rent has been paid for this month."

"But, Nicole..."

"My mind made up." Amy was cut off sharply.

The building was packed with dancing, eating, visiting people creating a general feeling of barely controlled chaos. Children ran in and out at will, oblivious to entreaties by parents to behave themselves and to not wander off. No formal reception line existed. Guests were left to approach the newlyweds and offer congratulations as they could. Some were introduced to the young couple's family, others were not depending solely on circumstances of the moment but everyone was having a good time. Nicole saw Richard's mother, Stephanie with her nondescript husband whose name she couldn't remember. Stephanie with unerring intuition had chosen to wear a long white skirt with light tan design with soft suede leather boots, also tan to match, and a white peasant blouse low off the shoulders, revealing her flawless tanned skin and the firm, comely, well formed, roundnesses of the mature woman.

With sparkling eyes and ready smile she was playing her role superbly with wit and charm. Nothing in her manner would indicate that she had not spent her entire life in the valley. Yes, Stephanie never did anything without confidence and flare. Certainly it was no accident that she was frequently near Wes and that she was very much aware, even as she ignored him, that his eyes strayed to her naked shoulders with which he no doubt had been so familiar. Perhaps it was Nicole's imagination that Stephanie had come prepared to taunt Wes, but she didn't think so. She was thoroughly irritated with the woman.

Later as Nicole circulated amongst the crowd, she noticed a group of people laughing together. There in the center with her back next to the wall. Sophi stood telling a story in her sweet little voice, accompanied by quaint gestures of her delicate shapely hands. With the innocent young girl quality ever present in her manner, she had mesmerized her friends. The story took an unexpected and funny twist at the very end and received an appreciative laugh.

Sophi had dressed in an elegant black evening gown that was really out of place in the valley, but the strength of her personality and charm quickly attracted her old friends about her, along with new admirers. She acknowledged Nicole with her eyes but continued immediately to tell another story. Nicole had been a little surprised to see Sophi at the wedding. She hadn't known Richard that well and hadn't seen Amy's family for some time, but as Nicole observed, Sophi's eyes discreetly flicked often in Wes' direction. Seeing Stephanie's husband whose name she couldn't remember sitting alone near the punch bowl, Nicole remembered the hospitality she had received in their home and went over to say hello.

"Hello, my dear. Let me get you a drink." Mr. Straussmen got carefully to his feet and brought her a glass.

"Good, isn't it?" he said after she had taken a sip.

"Yes, it is. Is this the first time you've been to our valley?"

"Yep. Pretty little place. I think I'll buy a house here and retire."

Nicole smiled at the irony of this statement. Stephanie had worked so hard to get out of this place. She noticed the malicious look on his face as he made this statement, even as Stephanie danced by.

"Do you dance?" Nicole offered.

"Not in my present condition," he grinned. "May I get you another drink?"

"I'm not done with this one."

Once again Straussmen carefully rose to his feet and went to the punch bowl and back.

"How is Millie?" Nicole asked after Richard's younger sister.

"She's here somewhere," he waved vaguely.

"Very well organized woman, my Stephanie," he commented as he watched his wife dance by with yet another man. "She never does anything without a good reason. She is not emotional and passionate, doesn't make dumb mistakes because of that like other women." Straussmen spoke to explain his wife's actions but his voice was morose. He knew as well as Nicole did that Stephanie was both emotional and passionate. Nicole guessed that the Straussmens had married to pursue a commonly perceived goal called success. Perhaps Stephanie's passion had been submerged to achieve her status but one look into her intelligent, lively eyes dispelled this concept completely.

Straussmen went for another drink. On each end of the table sat a large punch bowl. One contained champagne, the other a white grape juice mixed with seven up. Each bowl had lemon slices, and looked identical. Nicole, while she sat and visited with Straussmen, saw Millie visit the punch bowl regularly and dip out of the same bowl as her father. The boys of the valley had discovered her and kept her busy on the dance floor. The drinks seemed to liberate her movement and rhythm even as they seemed to petrify her father.

As the hour grew late, Wes dutifully danced with his son's bride, daughter Millie, ex number one, ex number two, wanna be number three, and promptly left. The newlyweds disappeared a short time later. Thirty minutes later the band announced they would play the last song. Immediately after the musicians began to put their instruments away there was a commotion at the south door.

"What's the matter?" Nicole stopped her mother and Roark as they hurried by.

"There's some problem with the cars."

Nicole hurried out to her car along with the others. Engines all over the parking lot were cranking vigorously but none would fire. Hoods were up and flash lights were probing the dark interiors, but to, no avail. The Pastor called the people back inside to decide what to do.

"It is very late. By the time we discover the problem and get all these vehicles running it would be morning anyway. May I suggest that we living here in town open our homes to friends and family from outer lying areas and those from distant places."

"I think we ought to call the sheriff's department," someone suggested.

"They are all here," he was informed.

"Isn't there a decent mechanic in town?" another asked. "I've got an important meeting tomorrow."

"He's asleep in the cloak roam, had too much to drink," came the reply.

Stephanie approached Nicole.

"We have reservations at the motel at the north end of the valley. I would make it well worth the proprietor's time if he would drive down and get us. In fact his motel might be empty if he doesn't."

"He is here too," Nicole informed her.

"I have a reservation there too." Sophi had come up in time to hear the bad news.

"The motel here in town is full and my friends are all related to Amy some way. Their homes are full." She looked hopefully at Nicole.

"Travis and the girls didn't come."

"My mother and her husband may need a place to stay and my place is awfully small," Nicole excused herself.

"Have you got a sleeping bag?" Sophi asked.

"We could call Wes. He has plenty of room. He left some time ago. I assume he made it all right."

"Definitely not," This from Stephanie.

"No, I guess not," Sophi concurred.

"Let me talk to Mom and see what can be worked out."

Nicole, with the two women in tow, located her mother.

"Roark and I are staying with his sister," Nicole was informed. There was nothing to do but invite the unwelcome guests home with her. Stephanie knew right, where to find her spouse. He was asleep in his chair near the empty punch bowl. A thorough search of the building and parking lot showed not a glimpse of Millie.

"I guess she will have to fend for herself," Stephanie finally gave up.

Stephanie and Nicole each took an arm and guided Mr. Straussmen down the street toward Nicole's.

"Wait up. These shoes are killing me," Sophi spoke from behind. They stopped and looked back as Sophi raised first one foot then the other and removed her shoes.

"You'll ruin your nylons," Stephanie observed. "Here, we'll shield you." Stephanie pulled her husband closer and turned to face the street. Nicole did the same on the other side forming a solid barrier against the eyes of the many other pedestrians walking about in the night. Sophi hiked her dress and removed her pantyhose.

"Ah, relief," she giggled.

Once they arrived from their four block walk Nicole explained the sleeping arrangements.

"The bedroom is at the end of the hall. There is a double bed for Stephanie and her husband. Sophi and I will have to sleep here on the hide-a-bed.'

"Go for it, dear," Stephanie pointed him

down the hall and gave him a firm shove. The befogged man stumbled down the dark passageway and through the door. Seconds later there was a crash.

"Oh!" Nicole exclaimed.   .   :

"He'll be alright," Stephanie declared. "I'll go take his shoes off so he won't get your bedspread dirty."

Stephanie returned shortly and sat down on the couch with a sigh. Sophi perched on the edge of the couch next to her. Stephanie pulled her skirt up onto her knees, raised a foot and began to tug on a boot with little result.

"Here," Nicole sat on the floor, seized the boot heel and toe and pulled it off. Stephanie raised the other foot and the other boot was removed.

"Thank you, dear." Stephanie took her boot from Nicole and pointed at a dark streak on the light tan leather.

"See that? Wes. It was like dancing with a work horse."

"I know what you mean," Sophi laughed.

Encouraged Stephanie continued.

"And did you see that suit he wore? Somber black, he looked like an undertaker." Wind blown from the walk home in the cool night breeze with the glow of the champagne still upon them, the two women made a pretty picture as they laughed at ol' Wes. With cheeks flushed and eyes gleaming with mischief Stephanie continued.

"He did one of his famous mispronunciations. You know in the western novels that he thinks are great literature, the cowboy always has a wry smile on his face?....He called it a 'Wire' smile!"

"Once he said he saw the coyote sillyhooted against the moon," Sophi contributed.

"Sillyhooted?"

"You know, silhouetted."

"Oh, hoooo!" The two women began to giggle uncontrollably.

"One time while at an art show, he called Gauguin, 'Gawkquin'! I thought I'd die!" Stephanie countered. Sophi laughed along with Stephanie although Nicole was sure that she wasn't familiar with the artist name either.

"I think he does it on purpose to make fun of intellectual snobs," Nicole opined.

"I wouldn't put it past him if he were smart enough," Stephanie countered. "His jokes are pretty juvenile. Oh, he can be charming IF he thinks about it. He can even be romantic IF he doesn't have a cow that is calving or he isn't involved in some stupid crusade. Tell her Sophi. You know how it was."

"I think Nicole has experienced it for herself from what I hear," Sophi responded.

"Been kinda rough on you has he dear?" Stephanie sympathized. "I hope you can understand what we are trying to tell you. There is no need to have you used up and cast aside like us old derelicts when you get a few more years on you."

Nicole smiled at the thought of these two lovely women being called derelicts.

"I've seen Wes act just like you say. He is not an easy man to deal with," Nicole confessed.

"Go ahead and smile. I was young and inexperienced. I could see nothing but a big, strong man who could protect and love me. Come to think of it when I look at Wes now I see nothing but a big, strong man, no brains, no finesse, no manners, ect." Stephanie laughed and was joined by Sophi's giggle.

"What do you see Sophi?" Stephanie was enjoying herself roasting Wes with Sophi's support.

"I see a man with an honest heart," Nicole interrupted.

Suddenly and without warning, Sophi began, to weep. The champagne had brought her emotions close to the surface, allowing her mood to swing to laughter with Stephanie, but her heart recognized the truth of Nicole's words.

She turned her back to the room and curled up in a ball and let the tears flow freely.

"What's the matter with her?!" Stephanie cried.

"Too much to drink."

"She is crying over that worthless bum we were married to!" Stephanie was suddenly very angry, her voice even becoming shrill.

"I think we should all go to bed," Nicole stood and waited for Stephanie to leave the room.

"You mark my words.... you wait and see... I don't want to have to say I told you so..." and other similar phrases were uttered in a constant stream until Stephanie herself shut the bedroom door.

Nicole urged Sophi aside until she made their bed, then she put her still weeping guest to bed as she would a small child. Finally the sniffles stopped and Sophi's breathing became even, only to be interrupted by a hiccup.

Nicole recognized that all the ridicule heaped upon Wes in such a sardonic, even humorous way by Stephanie, and the anger expressed when Sophi's true feelings were no longer suppressed, were evidence that Stephanie had been creating a smoke screen these many years to prevent her, from admitting she knew in her heart that her present husband who had fulfilled her every girlhood dream was a lesser man.

Poor Sophi had learned this hard lesson only a few months too late but had already accepted it. Stephanie' would spent her life justifying herself and heaping abuse upon Wes and not knowing what she was doing to herself and to her husband.

"And what about me?" Nicole asked herself. "Will I be the one to finally accept and love him the way he is or will I be the one who will never even have the opportunity to try?"

Morning brought normalcy to Nicole's little house. Once again Sophi was the lovely, carefully groomed, sophisticated, and self possessed, smiling creature of previous times, Stephanie, the epitome of confidence, graciousness, diplomacy and unerring social correctness.

Breakfast was cooked and served with a joint effort, the dishes washed, dried and put away. The scene played out in the wee hours of the morning was never mention or alluded to. Remembering Wes face smeared by her lipstick after her own over indulgence Nicole vowed to never mention the loosening of the tongues and the free flowing emotions induced by the over abundance of alcohol drunk by her guests. She also vowed to never touch the stuff again.

A deputy brought Millie by the house at mid-morning and escorted her in. She looked tired and sullen but as she was required to sit and listen to the deputy explain her all night absence, Nicole saw she was quite pleased with herself.

"Amy asked her brother and some of his teenage friends to switch the distributor wires on the cars of her friends that she thought might harass her. Once this was done she and Richard sneaked out and made their getaway. Of course when her friends tried to give chase they couldn't get their cars started. This little gal somehow got in on it. To the previous perpetrators as well as the victims, she suggested switching the distributor wires of all the cars in the entire parking lot out of pure mischief. Hardly a car in town would run last night as you well know."

"Well, young lady, what have you got to say for your self?" Stephanie quizzed her daughter.

"I was having a good time didn't want to go home."

"And where did you spend the night?"

"Around."

"With whom may I ask?"

"Friends."

"You make friends mighty easy. I suppose they were boys."

Millie shrugged.

"If you're going to embarrass me every time I take you somewhere, I'm going to leave you home."

The officer explained that there would be no charges filed. He also informed them that the mechanics in town were at that moment working to help people start their cars. Nicole's guests left soon after but not before properly expressing gratitude for the nights lodging. Nicole was tired. Despite the laughter and the gaiety, the wedding had been an ordeal for everyone on Wes' side of the family with the possible exception of Richard. Thank goodness it was over.

All the arrangements for a place to live and to get her into school had been made. Nicole had moved her things back to her mother's and cleaned the house for the new occupants. She had even gone over and helped Amy and Richard move in. She couldn't help thinking that it could have been her. Richard was already proving to be more responsible and attentive than Nicole had thought he could be. Had she been too hasty in not accepting Richard's offer? She decided that she hadn't, but still it was hard not to feel a little wistful. The newlyweds were still too full of their new closeness that pleasant intimacies bring to notice Nicole's mood.

For the last time Nicole sat in church with her two friends. Once again she had no interest in the sermon. She had sat up reading into the wee hours of the morning before she had been sleepy enough to fall into a restless sleep. There was no enthusiasm for the new adventure in Reno that was to begin the first thing in the morning. In fact, she preferred to think about nothing at all. She let the drowsiness overcome her and her head to slowly bow.

With a start, her head jerked up. Several people were looking at her. Embarrassed she sat straighter and looked up at the pastor, but sitting in the warm, quiet church coupled with her lethargic mood, drowsiness slowly overcame her once again.

This time she heard the soft snore that caused her head to jerk up. Again she noticed several people looking, some critically, some with a smile.

Wes! Suddenly she could feel him sitting behind her causing the hair to stand up on the back of her neck and goose bumps to rise on her arms, but she resisted the impulse to turn and look. After the services he fell in beside her as she moved up the aisle and out into the sun.

"May I give you a ride home?" he asked politely.

"I have my car here," she pointed out.

"Oh yeah," Long pause. "Nick, I have something I need to say."

"O.K.," Nicole waited.

Wes glanced around at the people passing them.

"Just between you and me," Long pause. "Maybe we could go for a drive."

Nicole nodded and walked toward his pickup with Wes so close on her heels that she was afraid he was going to step on her.

"Why are you following me?"

"I was going to open the door for you."

Sitting in his pickup as he drove she wondered why she was receiving the royal treatment, he had rarely held the door for her before. They drove out of town and headed west on a dirt road she had never been on before. Soon they climbed out of the valley onto the low hills and turned south. He parked or the edges of a steep incline both to the east and to the south. Automatically she got out before she realized that he had come around the truck to open the door for her.

She walked beside him to a large rock lying beneath a lone twisted juniper tree. He lifted his foot and placed it on the rock and leaned his elbows on a limb. As he gazed out over the valley the tension, in his face was slowly replaced with a serenity born of looking at something loved and cherished. Nicole suddenly recognized that they were standing above the swell through which they had driven Wes' cattle. The faint smell of rain on sagebrush came on a cool breath of air.

"I love that smell," Nicole sighed.

She remembered how she had hated this valley at first. Now as she looked out over the long narrow valley with its patched fields of alfalfa green and golden yellow stubble a lonely ache arose in her breast.

"I do too. Too bad it rains so seldom."

They stood together for a long time letting the peace of the moment engulf them.

"I hear you are leaving," Wes stated.

"Yes."

"Nick, I ah...You are a very lovely girl, woman." Wes began, still facing the valley.

"In your own quiet way," he continued as she too stood looking out over the valley, "you are a very capable, courageous and generous person. I want to thank you for all you've done to help me in my troubles. No man could know you and not want to be something special to you."

Nicole could feel the pulse beating in her neck. Did she dare hope? Could he be leading up to what she had hoped for, for so long?

Wes fell silent as if waiting, but then he went on.

"I am only a few years younger than your mother."

"And you sound Just like her!" Nicole thought harshly as she realized that she had followed the same strategy when she had tried to spare Richard's feeling, first the praise and then the goodbye. She determined that she would not show her disappointment as Richard had done.

"There is no denying that I still have feelings for Sophi which would have to be dealt with."

"I understand, Wes. There is no need to explain."

"I can't risk it. You must know the whole situation or I would somehow always feel I had deceived you. My financial situation is deteriorating. I'm still responsible legally and morally to my children. I no longer pay child support for Richard, but I do for the others."

"I know," Nicole tried to stop him.

"Only a few of the people in the valley consider me as a friend. I have no social life."

"I know."

"There are very powerful people who believe that our rights are political and are granted by government. I will never accept that premise. The great progress of the western world is based on the Judaic-Christian belief that we get our rights from our creator. I and my ideas stand in the path of those who would use government for their own aggrandizement. You've seen the results of that but I can't in good conscience give up the fight."

Nicole knew that too, it was for these reasons she admired him so, but the ache in her throat and the sting in her eyes caused from her effort to control her emotions kept her from speaking. She turned her face away.

"I've hardly taken the time to remember which fork to use when out in public. I have little culture or refinement. The only thing I know is how to make water run down through the alfalfa patch and what the ass end of a cow looks like and I may even lose the freedom to ranch. Sophi never received a store bought flower from ..."

"Shut up, Wes!"

Wes during the whole time had never taken his eyes from the valley and Nicole now stood with her back to him her face taut to control her emotions. After a considerable time Wes emitted a ragged sigh.

"Those are the realities of the situation."

Nicole only nodded, her control slipping, tears tricking.

"Raising our children won't be an easy row to hoe."

"Pardon me?"

Wes turned, placed his hands on her shoulders and pulled her gently to him. She could feel him shaking ever so slightly.

"I'm asking you to be my wife."

Nicole bowed her head and sobbed quietly for a few moments then twirled and buried her face in his chest. Wes patted her, reminding her of the first time she had hugged him and declared her love. She laughed even while she cried as she realized that Wes didn't know how to deal with a crying woman nor did he know how to interpret her actions.

"Yes, Sweetheart!"

The End

www.ingramcontent.com/pod-product-compliance
Lightning Source LLC
Chambersburg PA
CBHW031217020726
47499CB00002B/621